"Yegor" The Dudnik Circle #2
By Esther E. Schmidt

Yegor might be considered a dark romance.
So a warning comes with this book. It's not a typical light
and fluffy, it's closer to a dark and twisty romance.

Yegor is not intended for readers under the age of 18, and
anyone who is unable to read books containing, kidnapping,
murder, and assault. Do not read if sexual situations,
violence and explicit language offends you.

Cover design by:
Esther E. Schmidt

Model / Photographer:
Golden Czermak / FuriousFotog

facebook.com/FuriousFotog
instagram.com/furiousfotog
onefuriousfotog.com

CHRISTI DURBIN

Duuuuuuude….

"…the reason we work so damn well together.
Always on the same wave length,
like we share a brain."

Just some words in this book,
and yet…It's us.

GOLDEN CZERMAK

You give me what I need,
and if you don't have it…
you'll hunt it down and capture it.
Perfect visuals to compliment my stories.
Thanks for gracing this one
with that toned body of yours. Perfect!

Dear readers, this model/photographer
is also an amazing author.

Be sure to check out his books:
facebook.com/AuthorGoldenCzermak

CHAPTER ONE

Please, finish that sentence.

YEGOR

Shit. Glancing at my phone, I see the alarm is still active. I tear my gaze from the screen sitting on the passenger seat of my cocaine white Lamborghini Huracán LP 610-4 Spyder to focus on the road in front of me. I'm still two minutes out, dammit... hang in there, Ruby...I'm coming.

I pull up to the gate guarding my home and enter the code into the keypad. I can barely keep my shit together as it begins to swing open. The wheels of my car spin in the direction of my front door the moment I've got an inch of space on either side of my mirrors.

My mansion comes into view, and I see two doors are wide open: the entry into my home, and the driver's side door of my Mercedes GL550, which is parked in the driveway. Fuck. This doesn't look good.

For the last few weeks, I've been living in a spare room at my boss' place, because Ruby is living in my house. Who is Ruby? She's the girl I saved from the clutches of a gang who dealt in drugs and other bad shit, like kidnapping women and using them to make snuff movies.

The moment I laid eyes on her, lying in a bed with an IV in her arm, I knew. I felt it in my bones she was meant for me. But, some fucked-up circumstances followed my gallant rescue, ripping us apart. By this I mean I had to do my job as the second-in-command in the Dudnik Circle. Some necessary actions resulted in me breaking her trust. It was those circumstances that got in the way of claiming her as mine.

She has no one left in this world. We did a background check the day we rescued her. Ruby's parents died when she was little. She was thrown into the system and was bounced around until she was standing on her own two feet. Working her ass off to earn enough cash to keep going. Clearly not enough, because in the end, she lost her apartment.

I made the decision to give her the keys to my house. I made that choice because I had to know she'd be safe. Like I said; that was the only way I knew she had a roof over her head, and a secure one at that. I even monitor the house with an app on my phone that's connected to my security system. I like to be informed. I need to know if and when something is up.

That something is now. The fucking alarm went off seven minutes ago, and I broke a land speed record to get here as soon as possible. Jumping out of my car with my Glock in hand, I bolt for the door. Silently, I sneak my way through the foyer.

A few bags of groceries are strewn across the floor. Ice races through my veins when I spot shards of glass shattered all over. I hear water running in the other room, and I follow the drops of blood trailing in that direction.

I'm dodging pickles on the granite tiles beneath my feet to get into my own fucking kitchen. Shaking my head at the floor I glance up and that's when I see her. Ruby is bent over the sink, holding her hand underneath streaming water. Her head is turned away from both me and her hand.

"What the hell happened?" I growl.

She spins around and yanks her hand out from under the water. Now I can fucking see the cause of the mess everywhere. A piece of glass is jammed in her hand, sticking out far enough to see it from across the room.

"Oh, Little Spitfire." My voice softens as I place my Glock on the kitchen counter and stalk toward her.

Ruby's face is pale but her eyes indicate she's

glad to see me. Thank fuck, considering she's been fighting me ever since I betrayed her trust. My hands cup hers and I study the piece of glass that's lodged in her palm. Doesn't seem to be in there that deep, but damn, what the hell do I know?

I reach for my phone, only to find it's not in my pocket. Dammit, I must have left it in my car. The sound of footsteps reach my ears, and I'm immediately on edge. Spinning around, I grab my Glock in a fluid motion only to find the one I'm holding at gunpoint is none other than Nathan, the doctor for our gang; The Dudnik Circle.

"Mind aiming the pointy end somewhere else?" The idiot doesn't even appear to be scared. Hell, he looks close to rolling his eyes.

"What the hell are you doing here?" I spit back, not moving an inch.

Ruby's sweet voice flows from behind me. "I called him, Studly. Can you please let him help me now?"

Dammit. I can't think straight when there are guys around her. Especially Nathan. How the fuck can she call him and not me? *Because he's a fucking doctor, that's why.* But for real, she hated him for giving her a sedative. Okay, I asked him to, and that's why she hates me more.

When we saved her, she had been drugged. Hours later, I stooped to the same level by giving her something to make her sleep against her will. It was necessary for the circumstances and done without malice. She was still adjusting from being rescued out of the hands of those snuff film making scumbags, who kept Ruby's mind numb by drugging her.

When I found Ruby, she latched on and wouldn't let go. I needed to handle a life or death situation that involved my boss and I *had no other fucking choice.* Ruby was freaking out and wouldn't calm down. I am second-in-command and needed to leave but I had to keep her safe and handle things at the same time. So yeah, I lowered myself to scumbag level and ordered Nathan to sedate her. Knowing it would screw up my chances for a future with her.

It doesn't mean shit that I did it to protect her, so I could go after that same fucking gang who'd kidnapped her. We wiped the whole gang out, once and for all, so she won't have to look over her shoulder for the rest of her life.

With resentment, I holster my Glock and let Nathan pass. He places his bag on the kitchen counter and reaches for her hand.

"I'm gonna go grab my phone from my car." I mumble as I walk out, putting distance between us, because dammit, I might shoot the guy for touching her.

Even though the contact is meant to help, my mind can't seem to tell the difference. She's mine... except she isn't, because we're not together. She's still holding a grudge, and I respect that. I knew I blew my shot with her the moment that needle entered her skin. I sound like a broken record, but shit...I only did it because *I wanted to protect her*.

She may not think she needs me now but I sure as fuck will be there for whatever she may need in life. Like I said, my mind can't tell the difference. I'm hers, whether she wants me or not.

After I've closed the doors of both cars and calmed a bit, I walk back inside the mansion. I tuck my phone inside my pocket and saunter through the hallway. I can hear them talking softly and see Nathan close his bag as I approach.

"That was the last set of results we were waiting on. You're all clean and in the clear. Well, as long as you don't do anything foolish, like try to catch pickles in a jar that exploded, and you'll live." Nathan chuckles.

"What the fuck are you talking about, in the clear?" They both stare at me and their expressions indicate it's something they kept from me.

Nathan speaks first as he walks past me. "Medical shit, Yegor. She wanted a full rundown. Like a woman gets when she might have been raped."

My vision flashes red. In the blink of an eye, I grab his shirt and I spin him around. His back hits the wall as his bag slides across the kitchen floor.

I press my gun against his forehead. "Your hands were on her pussy?"

"Oh. My. God." Ruby gasps behind me.

"Stay out of this, Ruby." My voice is rough but I am trying to hold on.

"I'm a doctor, you idiot. I don't even see it like that. It's work." He fires back at me.

Preventing a fucking eye roll, my gaze stays locked. "Oh, yeah? So you never bury your cock in one? Slide your fucking tongue through it to taste sweet cum after you make a chick tremble through her orgasm?"

"Oh. My. God." Her voice trembles, but it's surely not from being afraid I might pop a round in the doc's head.

"Stop fucking saying that, Little Spitfire. Especially when it's laced with fucking awe, dammit." I growl while my hand starts to tremble.

Hell, with Ruby's history? How the fuck can she be turned on by my fucking words while I'm holding a guy at gunpoint?

"You will never put your hands on her again. Am I clear?" My voice is deadly.

The idiot chuckles. Chuckles. I push myself off him in one swift move, creating more space between us. I raise my aim slightly, and fire a round, inches from his head. "Am I making myself clear right fucking now?"

The dude steps away from the wall and looks behind him. "Yeah, I think you made your point... or hole, for that matter."

The fucker still thinks it's all a joke? The next second, a shot rings out and he drops to the floor, holding his leg. Yeah, totally nailed a bullet in the idiot who thinks I'm not serious.

"Fucking idiot! You're one of the most..."

I take aim right between his eyes. "Please, finish that sentence."

"Well, never fucking mind now. Give me my damn bag, asshole." Even though he's in obvious pain, he glares at me.

Ruby appears next to him with his bag and crouches down. A flash of fear trails in Nathan's eyes. Yeah, fucker, glad to see my message came across this time.

"Thank you, Jude. Now step away, please." Nathan averts his eyes and starts to patch himself up.

Double points for the fucker, backing off, calling my woman by her birth name, Jude. Not Ruby, the one I gave her, because she's got the brightest ruby-red hair. I know it's dye, but who the hell cares? It suits her fucking perfectly. With her pale skin and those bright green eyes that show just a hint of gray, it really stands out.

He finds his phone and brings it to his ear. "Can you drop by Yegor's place and come get me? No, I fucking can't….just come here and you'll see…. fine."

He drops the phone in his bag and leans his head against the wall. "You need to tell him, Jude. Clearly, you have to step over the issues you hold against him and let him in. You know that, right?"

I throw a glance over my shoulder and I find her studying the floor.

"I know…and I will. I see that now." Ruby releases a deep breath.

"So thankful to help out, you know…by taking a freaking bullet in the leg. Took you long enough to realize it's him you need to turn to." Nathan grumbles with his eyes closed.

The fucker is lucky I already shot him and he can't see the tear sliding off Ruby's pale cheek. Stepping forward, I risk rejection and pull her against my chest. The way we've been firing off arguments at each other, there's a possibility she'll kick me in the nuts or punch me in the face, but I will take that chance. She's got an injured hand, and she's fucking crying. I'm unable to resist.

Ruby doesn't return the hug, but she lays her head against my chest and leans into me. My heartstrings tug. I should never have given her space. Even if it meant that she would hate me more than she already does. I regret stepping away for those few weeks.

Clearly, there's something going on beyond dropping pickles and cutting her hand in the process.

"Come on, Ruby. If you can make some coffee or tea or some shit, I'll clean up the hallway." I murmur against her hair.

Squeezing her once more, I regretfully step away. She doesn't even grace me with one word but walks to the stove and grabs a little pan sitting on an unlit burner. Holding it under the tap, she fills it with water.

"What are you doing?" I wonder out loud. Because usually, one would either make coffee with the machine or use the kettle for tea.

"Making ginger tea." She throws over her shoulder.

Ginger tea. That shit burns in your throat. I shake my head and walk towards the closet to get a broom and start cleaning up the shards of glass in the foyer. I have a cleaning company come by twice a week, but that doesn't mean I don't know how to do things myself.

Normally, when I'm called in to clean up a mess…I make it even worse before everything becomes squeaky clean. But that type of cleaning involves bodies instead of pickles.

It doesn't take long before I see Ford walking into my house with his wife, Tarzan, close behind. "Mind telling me why Nathan called me to come get him?"

"Probably 'cause I shot the fucker in the leg." I shrug, not feeling remorseful in the least.

Ford snorts. "Just the leg, huh? Lucky. Where's he at?"

See? That's why he's the boss and I'm his right hand. Our background runs deep. Hell, he didn't even care that I wasn't full-blood Russian when he made me second-in-command. Trust isn't a word, it's something that's rooted deep into your whole being. It's built up through years, with actions, behavior, and shit like that. That's why he doesn't question my motivation.

And yeah, the fucker is lucky. I always aim for the head when my Glock comes to play. "Kitchen."

My boss, the head of the Dudnik Circle, strolls toward my kitchen.

Tarzan's gaze hits mine. "Ruby okay?"

Again...see? I don't mind Tarzan calling her Ruby. Tarzan is one hell of a tough woman and also my boss. Her gang merged with ours and instead of choosing a leader, we have two. Yes, Tarzan was the head of her own gang. She's damn impressive with ropes too so don't get on her bad side.

"She dropped a glass jar and cut her hand. I have a feeling something's up though because Nathan was talking to her, and I kinda flipped when he mentioned something about test results." My hands disappear into my pockets.

Tarzan steps closer and drops her voice. "Lock up your weapons and the door, be sure to hand Ruby the keys when she starts to talk...and fucking listen to what she has to tell you, okay? Keep calm. That's all I'm gonna say."

Fuck. That's two damn people she talked to about whatever it is that she's keeping from me. Tarzan and

Nathan. Not me. Fury starts to build inside my body, piling up and flowing through my veins.

"Keep calm." Tarzan repeats in a fucking sing-song tune before she goes in search of her husband.

I've been standing on the fucking sideline for what feels like forever. Giving her space, and now I wonder why. Keep. Calm. Calm. Can you eat it that shit? No. Then why the fuck should I keep it then?

CHAPTER TWO

You game?

Ruby

My hand still throbs where the piece of glass had been lodged. I'm so angry at myself for flipping out. All because of a piece of paper that was stuck underneath the windshield wiper of my car. For crying out loud, it was nothing. Pure silliness. I mean for real, advertising leads to a full-blown panic attack?

Okay, it did state *'I will find you'*. That's the only thing my mind processed and I jumped to the conclusion that the ones who kidnapped me placed it there. Instead, it was just an advertisement for some kind of app for finding shit, missing persons, family members, partners, or kids that need tracking. I'm losing my mind.

There I was, hightailing it home from the store with my hands shaking the whole way. That's when I couldn't catch my breath and the black spots appeared in my vision. I was running inside and dropped the pickles. Mindlessly I started picking up the shards…mental note: don't be distracted when picking up sharp objects.

As a result I have the one person around me that I can't have near me: Yegor. I know for certain he can and will keep me safe, but on the other hand, I can't let myself trust anyone ever again.

Yegor made me feel safe when he dragged me out of the place they kept me prisoner. I had been kidnapped, tied to a bed, and drugged when he found me. I can remember his voice…one word, and they followed his command. He was there *for me*. Call it a gut feeling, instinct, whatever…even when I was out of it, his voice, his scent, his embrace, everything enveloped me into a secure, empowering web.

Then he chose to drug me up. Yes, to keep me safe…I knew and understood that when I was calm enough to think clearly. But it was another stab in the back; a token to never put myself out there again. I needed to protect myself from any emotion or influence. I couldn't be near the guy who in such a short time forged a deep connection.

I didn't even know him at all, and yet it was like our souls recognized their counterparts. Distance. I needed it to build the walls around my heart. I pushed him away but he gave me the keys to his mansion and demanded I stay there. A top of the line security system and everything I needed to get back on my feet.

I had no other option but to accept. Why? Some details are still fuzzy, but I know with one hundred percent certainty that the fucker who had me kidnapped is still out there looking for me. How do I know this? Because he was supposed to come for me, they were saving me for him. That, and I was about to lose my apartment when I was taken. So now I have absolutely nothing. Brought up in foster care, I have no family to turn to, no house, hell...I don't even have clothes.

Tarzan, Ford's wife, has become a good friend. She made sure I settled into Yegor's house and gave me some of her clothes. Yegor set up a bank account for me with unlimited funds but I refuse to touch it. I'm imposing enough on him as it is. I don't want to take his money.

I've been helping Tarzan with some administrative things. She said she needed my help and offered to pay me in return. I know she did it because she knew I needed money for groceries and I wanted to earn it myself. I can't thank her enough for being there for me.

Truth be told, I haven't completely opened up to Tarzan. I'm pretty sure she's aware of it, and yet she still treats me like her best friend. No judgment whatsoever. She is even teaching me how to defend myself.

This has also helped me to relieve some stress. Both from the hard, driven, workout…and from the knowledge I can now kick someone's ass.

During those training sessions, she curses a lot in Russian. That led me to ask her to teach me that as well. With all these Russian guys around me, it might come in handy to know what the hell they are saying especially when they bark out orders.

I asked Tarzan if Nathan, the doctor, could be trusted. She said she trusted him with her life. She offered to be right there with me when I asked Nathan to do something for me. There were some holes in my memory and to keep myself sane, I needed him to run some medical tests and listen so I could talk things through.

I was hoping to piece together what happened. Or at least cross some stuff off my list of things that had me freaking out, so I could struggle my way through it. I need to process what happened, then set my eyes on the future.

It turns out I wasn't raped. On one hand, it was a relief I was still a virgin, and on the other, slight panic. I'm still freaking out over the idiot who had me kidnapped, who wanted to rape and kill me. I don't even know the jackass or why he was dead set on getting me.

Yegor said he and the gang wiped out every-one responsible. But since I was still on that bed, drugged, I was sure the jackass wasn't killed when they rescued me or went back for revenge. Let's just state that he never got the chance to pick up the package that he ordered. Me being the package, him placing the order, anonymously.

Well, not so much anonymous, because the only thing I know is his name. How do I know this? Be-cause the guys that took me kept repeating the same thing over and over again. He's coming for you. Paco Hurtado wants to fuck your cunt and slice your neck. A chill prickles my skin because the memory is so vivid.

"Are you cold? Hungry? Need to lie down? What do you need, Ruby?" Yegor asks while he scans my body with those hawk eyes of his.

And yet another reason I need to keep him away from me. He seems to see everything, read my mind, or my body for that matter. I can't lie or hold anything back from him. I need to get this over with. Hiding, running, avoiding hasn't gotten me anywhere.

I need to face this head on. Go after the fucker who screwed with my life. Nathan and Tarzan both stressed that I needed to tell Yegor because he would move heaven and earth for me. I didn't want to dump my problems on him, though.

Except, how I just witnessed him shooting Nathan in the leg because he performed a medical procedure on me? Yes, somehow I don't think he would be bothered to track down the man who wanted to rape and kill me.

"What I need is to get laid." Yes. That would definitely cross off the virgin part, so the next one on the list would be, "And then kill someone. You game?"

Okay, I'm not sure what I was thinking or what I expected when I voiced my thoughts just now…but the sly smile that is spreading slowly on his lips is both creepy and sexy as hell.

His head tilts to the left, a twinkle in his eyes. "In that order, Little Spitfire?"

"Yes, because if I fail to kill him, he might find me again and rape me because he wants my virginity. So yes, it needs to be in that order." I'm agitated, mostly at myself and how I'm handling things.

Because he wants my virginity. Why did I have to blurt it out like that? Ugh, why didn't I have sex a long time ago? Maybe then all of this would have never happened. I've been trying to wrap my mind around the fact how this guy found out I was a virgin. I mean it's not like I placed an ad or have it written on my forehead or something.

Maybe it had something to do with making sure no one would touch me because he would know if they did. Doesn't matter, I need to take care of it. It meaning getting laid and be gone with the virgin part.

Dammit. I should have had this talk a whole different way. With some reason, using my mind, sitting down, and explaining things more thoroughly instead of getting straight to the end game. Ugh, I'm an idiot, and now he's shocked. Not from the rape part, but the second the word virginity crossed my lips, he actually took a step back.

"Great. Mr. ImmaShootYourLegBecauseYouTouchedHerPussy. You look like you're ready to run away from me. Go on, fuck off then." I cross my arms in front of my chest and the instant I do, I regret it due to the slicing pain in my hand. Dammit. My breath hisses out between my teeth.

Yegor closes the distance between us and cradles my hand in his. "Calm down there, hellion. I'd kill for you, no questions asked. I'd whip out my gun and spit a bullet right between the eyes. The virgin part we need to discuss before I whip out my dick and spit cum. Clear?"

"Christ. Take a life, no prob...take someone's virginity, who's willingly giving it to you, by the way,… hang on, because I don't want to taint my conscience. You're weird." And too freaking close.

"Just weird? That's what you're going with?" He whispers against my neck while his nose brushes along my skin.

A strangled noise leaves my lips because really… I have no words. I know I asked him to have sex, but that's just shove it in, bounce it around, exchange fluids, and done, right? I mean it's nothing like what I've read in books, all romantic and mind blowing. Fiction and reality can be quite the contradiction.

His hand snakes up my arm, around my neck, and when I feel his fingers tighten in my hair, he murmurs in my ear, "Give me the name, Ruby. The one we're going to kill…together."

I don't even think; I just breathe out the name. "Paco Hurtado."

Yegor inhales sharply, his whole body goes rigid.

I've kept Paco's name from both Nathan and Tarzan. No matter what, I want to be the one who kills him. I need to do this myself.

Except, like I mentioned before, I can't resist Yegor, and I know without a doubt he would do anything for me.

And here it comes. The guilt that slices through my heart. Am I using him? I don't know. It's confusing. Feelings of revenge, hurt, anger…and shit, if he keeps rubbing against me, desire will push every inch of guilt aside.

It's for that reason my body rocks back against him, and I feel something hard pressing between us. With a growl that rips from his lips, and a bite of pain in my scalp, my head is yanked to the side by the fist in my hair as his mouth slams down on mine.

My teeth capture his tongue that's brutally dominating my mouth. I might be a virgin, but I've been kissed once or twice, and those times don't compare to what Yegor is doing. He doesn't kiss…he dominates and hungrily seeks the best strategy to devour me.

He manages to chuckle against my mouth while I've still got his tongue pinned between my teeth, tightening before I let go. I try to gather some distance between us, but his hand is still lodged in my hair, keeping my head in place, his body flush against mine.

"Have you finally come to the understanding why I said we need to talk about the fucking first, Ruby? Because you need to realize it will take a little more than shoving my dick through your hymen. It involves mouth fucking, finger fucking, tongue fucking, pussy fucking, dick fucking, and on occasion even some ass fucking. That all depends on what I'm in the mood for and what my woman wants or needs. Sometimes, that isn't your decision. I'm not an easy man to please, Ruby. I demand and take." With his fingers clenched tight in my hair, his other hand slides over my neck and grabs my jaw. "Make no mistake, you are my woman. But first we need to settle some things. Then, I will claim you with my dick, and after we both get our fill, I'll start the hunt for Paco Hurtado."

Damn. I should be terrified, and yet I can't wait for this man to stop talking and show me his intentions. His words are doing crazy things to my body. My nipples tighten and my resolve strengthens. I'm done pushing him away.

These past few weeks have been hell and standing here in this very moment...the place between my legs throbs as heat flows through my body. I feel alive. Somehow, the thought of using him to either gain my revenge or ensure my safety falls away. I want to be claimed by him, as his woman.

His inked hand tightens around my jaw. "Are my words sinking in, Little Spitfire?"

Swallowing, I gather all my strength and lean into his tight grip. "Done with the talk now, Studly? Because I'm ready for something else to sink in."

"Woman. I have been ready since the day I saw you lying on that bed all drugged up. Now that might sound fucked up, and it really is, but right fucking now...I need to decline." His upper lip curls up in a snarl of disgust.

"No." Gasping, I realize the mistake I made.

Pushing him away, and then throwing myself at him to demand he fuck and kill for me. I'm disgusted with myself. I want to close my eyes, sag down in misery, and crumble to the ground. Except, that was the old me, before Paco Hurtado ordered his men to kidnap me so he could rape and kill me.

There's no time for self-pity, and the throbbing in my hand is a reminder I don't want to live in fear anymore. It's time for a hunt, tables are meant to be turned. No more freaking deer. I am the hunter. Beware, Paco Hurtado...I am coming for you.

I push against Yegor's chest. He lets me, but only the hand in my hair falls away, while he keeps the one on my jaw in place. Fine, fucker. Watch me. I wrap my good hand around his wrist while my other hand goes to his face. In one swift move, I push his head back, rotate my body, and throw my elbow over the arm that's gripping my jaw.

His back is bent due to the pressure of the un-natural angle of his arm, and this allows me to pound my fist on his back. I immediately regret the move, because it's the hand that's throbbing from the glass cut.

Screaming out my frustrations, I step away from Yegor, who is clearly shocked. Eyes bulged, his eyebrows arch up a notch before lowering in confusion.

Straightening his back, he steps in my direction. "First, you're going to tell me why the fuck you did that just now, and then you're going to fucking tell me where the hell you learned that shit."

Why do I get the vibe that he allowed me to fight him off? Because he looks like he's ready to fight an army of trained men to get an answer. Shit. He shot Nathan because he touched me. Even though it was medically necessary, that didn't keep him from putting a bullet in Nathan's leg.

"Why? So you can shoot the person who helped me learn to defend myself?" I seethe.

"Depends." He growls back.

"On what?" I snap.

"Just fucking tell me so I can decide." Yegor barks.

Thinking about it, I have nothing to hide. I'd put my money on Tarzan any day. She could totally kick his ass. Or at least give it a good shot. "Tarzan."

His eyebrows raise and his head bobs in appreciation. "Nice. But that shit stops right now. I'll be training you."

I step in his direction and jab a finger in his chest. "Not gonna happen. I don't need anything from you. I will handle everything myself."

Yegor curses and mumbles under his breath in Russian. "The only fucking woman I need more than life itself, and she keeps pushing me away."

Okay, I know for a fact he switched to Russian so I couldn't understand what he said. Well, shit-for-brains screwed that one up real good, underestimating me like that. "I wasn't pushing you away a moment ago, now was I? You were disgusted by my offer. Maybe rightfully so, but..."

And...his fingers curl around my jaw again. His eyes are flaming and anger visibly rolls off him. "You understand Russian? Who?"

I roll my eyes. "You and your freaking who all the time. Why does it bother you when anyone does stuff with me? Jesus..."

"Ruby." His voice is more of a raw grumbling sound instead of my name. "Clearly, my words didn't sink in when I said you are my woman. Mine. Which fucking means I know everything that involves you and your every need. I wasn't disgusted by you, for fuck's sake. I was disgusted at myself, because all I want to do is lower my zipper and sink inside that tight pussy of yours. And I have no doubt it will be tight. Get my drift? I don't even want to bother with undressing. That isn't something you need for the first time. It won't be pleasant, Ruby. My dick is going to hurt you the first time before it's able to bring you a future of intense pleasure. So, you're going to be lying on a bed with me worshipping your body with my mouth for a long time. That way you'll be begging, craving me, to hurt you. Fuck. Let's start in the shower so my hands can roam every inch of you first."

"Okay." That single word slips past my lips. My whole body is already longing and ready to beg, due to the promise in his statement.

Virgin or not, I've read enough smut to know what the roaming of hands will entail. I can't wait to do the same, to touch him, taste him, and take him into my mouth. I'm curious and filled with anticipation.

The place between my legs throbs and so does my hand, each in different ways. My gaze dips to my hand to see why it's hurting. Blood is seeping right through the bandage Nathan put on earlier.

Yegor's head drops and his hand falls away from my jaw. "Fuck. We need to take a look at this." He starts to drag me along with him.

"Might have to skip the fucking shower." He grumbles in Russian.

"Da." I don't know why, but it's out before I realized I agreed in his language.

He spins on his heel and leans close to my face. "I fucking love the fact that you understand my native language. But I need to focus on taking care of you in a whole different way, and with you speaking Russian? Even if it's only one fucking word, you have me on the brink of throwing my resistance overboard and fucking you right here. So please, for the love of all that is holy, or just your hymen for that matter, zip it and let's get that bleeding stopped before my dick draws blood."

"Okay." Again, I can only reply with just one single word.

I say it in English, because I don't want to risk poking the bear some more, because he's obviously on edge. There's no other choice at this point. I've come to the understanding and realization that there's only one single option here. It's time to give him the reins.

CHAPTER THREE

Excuse my wife.

YEGOR

My phone chimes with an incoming message. Reaching in my pocket, I drag it out of my black slacks and check the screen and see it's from Ford, my boss. He's letting me know there's a meeting set for eleven at his house.

Normally, I'd be at Ford's house in one of the rooms upstairs. All of my shit is there, at least since I moved Ruby into my mansion. Seeing how things went down today, though, all that has changed.

There's no fucking way I'm staying away from her again.

Before Ford and Tarzan had dragged Nathan out of my house, I requested a meeting. Although he backs me up with no questions asked, that doesn't mean I get off without some blowback for putting a bullet into the leg of one of our own men.

I'm glad the meeting is set so I can jump into action to hunt down Paco Hurtado. Fucking Paco. Why did it have to be him? Out of all the goddamned people in this godforsaken world. No matter how black my past is, he seems to darken it even more. I need to get things handled before someone tells him where Ruby is.

Yes, I know damn well who Paco is. Never in a million years did I think that name, or that fucker, would cross my brain, or my path. I lead a different life now, one where I'm part of a Russian gang. I have a messy past, not to mention a messed up family tree. I might have been given a Russian name, raised as a Russian, but one look and you can tell my Italian heritage.

Over twenty years ago there was a forced truce between our families. Yes, I'm talking about family in the sense of gangs here. Meaning they stopped fighting and steer clear from one another from then on. Well…on this account I'd say fuck the truce, I'm going to kill him on the spot.

But there's one very fucking tiny bright side to all of this. I'm pretty sure Ruby's not going to like it, but again…I don't give a fuck. She's going to hate me either way. Here I thought I'd fucked up a few weeks ago, but throw Paco in the mix? Yeah, I might need to find the solution for hell to freeze over if I ever think there'll be a future for the two of us.

I shoot another message to my lawyer before I place my phone into my back pocket. Ruby strolls into the living room. We put a new bandage on her hand a moment ago, and she'd walked off to put the first aid kit away.

Damn lucky we needed to change that bandage too, because all I want to do is devour her. Any damn way I can. And I can't due to the fact that my soul is as dark as my fucking. So I need space.

"Sit." I snap.

I'm on edge and it's better to get the whole thing out of the way first so we can move forward. *Getting to the 'need for her to hate me' part.* Believe me; it's better this way.

She takes a seat across from me. To give myself another minute to calm down, I glance around the room. This house's got a huge living room with a big enough fireplace I could stand in it. Hell, I could burn a fucking body in it. Except the stench would draw people over, so that's a no go.

The term 'I see red' is something that suits me on more than one account. My whole living room is dark red: the ceiling, walls, floors, furniture, every-fucking-thing. I like it that way. It's rich, warm, and it soothes me. Drawing on the soothing quality, I turn back to Ruby.

Before I can utter another word, she slides off her chair and crawls seductively my way. What. The. Fuck? When she reaches me, her hand slides up my leg and heads straight for my dick. I shake my head because fuck…that's been my wet dream for the last few weeks. *On her knees and my dick in her mouth.*

When her fingers tighten around the growing bulge in my slacks and squeeze, I fucking know it's reality. The groan that leaves my mouth rumbles through my chest and is damn loud even to my own ears. Seeing she's going to hate me anyway, it's better to add to the fire. Show her a hint of the domination I demand when it involves my dick.

I slide my fingers into her hair and pull her head back. "You want a little taste, Little Spitfire? Open the fucking zipper."

Ruby's eyes stay on mine as she pulls it down. She wants to reach for my cock, but that's where she's wrong. The hand I had wrapped in her hair slides to the side, so I cup her neck underneath her jaw and guide her cheek against my leg, *putting her in place.*

My other hand whips out my dick and I stroke it in front of her. Letting her enjoy the view of my cock. She's got no other fucking option but to use her eyes, because I've got her pinned between my hand and my hip. Looking down at the sight before me, my knees almost buckle at the intense visual.

Every pump she matches with a gasp, as though she needs my cock in her mouth. Carnal hunger dances in her eyes. As I guide my dick a whisper from her lips, she opens her mouth fully. Fuck no, I'm not ready to give it to her yet. Her breath is scorching, but I'm the one in charge, and the second my tip enters that hot as sin mouth, my cum will coat her throat, so I'm stalling.

"You want to know who your man is, Ruby? The guy you asked to take your virginity? I'll fucking show you. You'll hate me for what comes next, but it's inevitable. In the end, life will always cause pain. It's the shit you have to endure to appreciate the good things that are scarcely thrown your way. Open up, Little Spitfire." I growl out that last part in a dark demand.

Her lips part as my hand reaches for the back of her head, keeping her in place, while I jam my cock deep inside her mouth. I pump at the base of my cock while I thrust my hips.

I feel her choke on my dick, didn't you get the hint yet? I'm a bastard, and I own that shit. "Swallow, Ruby. Fucking swallow my cock. Breathe through your fucking nose because I ain't pulling back. This is me fucking your mouth, and you're going to give me everything I demand. Fuck, yeah. That's it."

Tears are running down her cheeks and I'm in fucking heaven. That's right. I mentioned my soul is dark as well as my actions. This includes the way I fuck. She needs to know, needs to feel what it's like to belong to me.

Her moans are sending trembles through my cock. Normally, when I fuck a face, they grip my legs and try to push me off. It's the reason I started to blindfold them and bind their hands. None of this would be happening the way it's going down now if it was anyone other than Ruby. For one, I'm not wearing a rubber. And I always wrap up, no exceptions. Until now.

Second, I need to shake my head to clear it when I feel her moaning again around my dick. My gaze trails from her mouth taking my cock to her eyes. They are closed. A look of contentment spread over her face. Tilting my head, I see her hand tucked between her goddamned legs.

Dammit. I can't hold back. I feel my balls draw up. It's been too long; I haven't fucked a woman since I first laid eyes on Ruby. I've jerked off to this very dream that's now a reality. Her lips tighten around my mushroom head that's thickening even more.

Thrusting my hips, my fingers tighten in her hair, causing her to moan while her body shakes. She's fucking coming while hot streams of cum shoot down her throat. An animalistic sound rumbles through the air. I become lightheaded, while my body fills with a heavenly feeling that nobody has ever triggered inside me.

My chest is heaving, and I need to pull myself together. Fuck. Best blowjob ever combined with

Esther E. Schmidt

the fastest orgasm ever. It may have something to do with the fact I haven't had sex since the day I met her. Or it's her. Let's hope to fuck it's the first thing because a track record of mere minutes is not something I need. I'm dying to test that theory, though. Holy hell…that thought shooting through my brain while I just emptied myself. I'm hooked all right.

My dick leaves her mouth and the cold air reminds me that I failed to make her hate me. Because how the fuck would I have known this virgin would get herself off while I roughly fucked her mouth? I grab my cock and zip the fucker back up.

Plan fucking B. Instant hate, comin' right up. "Paco Hurtado is my brother."

Ruby's glassed over eyes flash in disbelief before she scrambles back. Yeah, that kinda sealed the deal, my fate, whatever.

"No…" She gasps.

Slowly nodding my head, I stand a little taller. Do not fucking sugarcoat that shit. "Oh, yeah. He is. Half-brother, same mother, shared DNA, that kind

57

of brother. No fucking denying it. Also the reason why…"

The doorbell rings, right on fucking time. I don't finish enlightening her further but step up to buzz in my lawyer.

That text I sent earlier? Yeah, I needed to get a marriage license filled out, paid for, add our valid IDs and settle all of the legal requirements, that shit. Thing is, I may have needed Ruby's 'I do,' although it wasn't really necessary. Us getting married is.

"Laura." My acknowledgment is curt.

Behind me, I sense Ruby storming up due to the gust of wind she manages to push forward with her speed. Glancing over my shoulder, I can tell by her fire-spitting-gaze she's ready to blow. Why…I have no…aw, fuck. How can she be jealous when I require her hate?

"You need to fucking leave." Ruby seethes. "We were in the middle of something, so get the hell out."

Laura ignores her completely and holds up a file for me to grab. "Here you go, all taken care of. Need anything else?"

"No. Yegor and I were busy, so not from you he doesn't," Ruby sneers. "Other than your exit strategy, because you are neither welcome nor wanted here."

Ruby crosses her arms in front of her chest and taps her fingers on her arm, pinning her laser glare on Laura.

I hold up the file in silent thanks.

"Excuse my wife. She just gave me a blowjob while she finger-fucked herself to orgasm." That statement makes Ruby's mouth drop.

Laura chuckles.

Shooting Ruby a wink, I add, "Looks like she's ready for round two."

"Well, seems like I'm not needed here, so I'm off to do something more useful." Laura doesn't even wait for a response. She turns to leave, and I shut the door behind her.

"You're insane." Ruby shakes her head. "And I'm not your wife." She bites out.

Opening the file, I grab a document and hold it

out for her to take. Her gaze scans over the words, making her eyes widen.

"Noooo." She gasps. "How can you do that? Is that even possible? We're not…how? No. Married?" Ruby squeaks.

"Come on. We need to talk." I take a step toward the living room.

Ruby rips away the file and starts smacking me on the head with it. What the fuck?

"What did you do? What did you do?" She chants while smacking the shit out of me with the damn papers.

Finding her wrists, I grab both and give her a light shake. "Stop, dammit. That's what I wanted to explain so follow me into the living room so I can do just that."

Ruby rips away from my hold and stomps the whole way. Fucking adorable and this amazing woman is all mine.

"We're here." Her arms wide, rocking left and right in half a circle. "Now you better damn well start talking, and fast. What is this bullshit?"

"Long or short version?" I ask.

She actually growls deep in her chest. "Short now, long version maybe later, if I don't kill you before that."

"Married a few minutes and already wants to be a widow." I murmur.

She stalks in my direction and she actually manages to make it feel like a threat. I maintain my cool, because I sure as fuck know she doesn't need laughter from me to provoke her.

I hold up my hands in a gesture of surrender. "My half-brother, from a different father, is Italian. There are laws, contracts, agreements, whatever you want to call it...between gangs; things everyone honors. Or should, for that matter. One of those is that wives are to be untouched." I can't help my distaste about that part, because I know all too well that there are people out there who say 'fuck the rules'. "Anyway...with you being a virgin and shit..." Damn, I need to take a breath or two to calm myself because there has never been so much hatred flooding my veins. Not even when...

Soft strokes on my arm make me open my eyes. I didn't even realize I'd closed them.

"Go on." Ruby's face holds no anger, instead, there's only worry.

For me? Damn…

Swallowing, I continue. "Paco's the head of an Italian gang. He wanted you untouched,"

Ruby shakes her head. "It doesn't make any sense, he wanted me untouched, yes…but they also said he would kill me. It's insane, I don't even know how he knew I was a virgin." Ruby gasps and steps back. "Shit…a virgin, you're talking about a tradition after marriage…showing the blood on the sheets." She grumbles.

"Yes." I growl in frustration because that's what the fucker was planning. I fucking know it.

"It's the same damn thing that happened with my mother. Except, she wasn't a virgin. She had me…" Shit. I shouldn't have said that part out loud.

Turning, I try to leave, and yet her words stop me. "As I have you."

My eyes fall shut again. Damn emotions. Ruby is supposed to hate me. That's the only way to keep her safe. Doesn't she understand what it all entails? This life….hell…life can be gone with your next breath… and yet…there's reason in those four words.

Spinning around to face her, I close the distance between us. "By law, in life until death, you'll have me."

CHAPTER FOUR

Place it on social media for all to see.

Ruby

I still can't believe I'm holding a piece of paper, well…not so much paper…a freaking marriage license. This is insane. Yet it's another thing he did to protect me. Slowly placing the paper on the table, I lean back against the couch.

I turn my head in his direction. "So Paco can't touch me now that I'm married to you."

It's not a question, because I know a little about the Italian mob…ugh…again, only from reading.

Like how I read about giving a blowjob...the way I was using my tongue and mouth on him... very productive information, if I do say so myself. Then again, it was more like a crash course taught by Yegor. Because the way he took over wasn't from any book I've read.

My cheeks flush at the reminder and I'm thankful his voice pulls me away from my thoughts. "It was the first thing that popped in my head, a short-term solution. You should have told me sooner. I have no doubt the news that you were freed from the hands of those snuff movie idiots has already reached him. That's why you panicked earlier, right? Because he's still after you, isn't he?"

I nod in agreement. It's time to tell him some more about what happened, so I might as well start from the beginning. "I worked as a secretary at a car dealership. My friend, Ava, she..." I have to swallow, because a memory flashes through my head that I need to bury. "She takes, took, side jobs. Ava was a waitress at these high-class cruise nights. She knows

…dammit… *knew*…I'd never…but I needed the cash, and she practically begged me not to let her go alone. So, I went with her and the moment we stepped foot on that ship…"

Yegor stands from the couch. "He planned it, even if you hadn't gone to that ship, he would have had you picked up anyway."

"Yeah, but then Ava would still be alive, now wouldn't she? Because it was me they wanted, not her. It's my fault. Her blood is on my hands." I don't mean to hurl the angry words at him but no one else is around.

"Never." He grunts back. "Don't ever fucking think that way."

"How can I not? They raped and killed her right in front of me, Yegor. I never should have…"

"What?" He snaps. "Never should have made friends? Never should have lived your life? What, Ruby? Because he's the one who slipped off track, not you. This whole pile of shit is on him and the fuckers involved. *Not you.*"

My chest is heaving and the words stumble through my mind and over my lips. "I want him dead."

"Soon." That one word from Yegor is a solid promise in my ears.

He checks his watch before his gaze lands back on mine. "I need to head over to Ford's place. There's a meeting, and I'm going to bring this matter up. He'll reach out to Paco so it's official and out in the open that you're not to be touched."

I step back. "No." I whisper. This means he's settling. Not killing, just protecting me. "You promised."

"We will get our revenge, Little Spitfire. I just need a fucking plan. But first, I'm taking the official route, through my boss. This is the only way to handle it correctly." He pins me with a gaze that only boils fury within me.

"Never mind," I sneer. "I'll handle my own problems. I wouldn't want to get you in any trouble with your boss."

Esther E. Schmidt

I can't help it. My jaw hurts from grinding my teeth. Spinning around, I head for the stairs. How could I have thought it would be him and me going after Paco? How could I drag him into this? Slamming the door shut behind me, I flip the lock and lean back. I hear and feel Yegor pound on the door before he checks the handle.

"Open the fucking door, Ruby." He bellows.

I pound my fists on the door to add some force to my words. "Leave me alone."

"Never. Open the fucking door or step away, because I'm going to kick it in, Ruby."

Flipping the lock, I swing the door open. "Just go, okay? Rewind the last few hours and go back to Ford. I can't…."

His fingers wrap around my throat while he lowers his face to mine. "No, we can't. Believe me when I say I want nothing more than to hunt Paco down and kill him on the fucking spot. But before I get to that point, I need to go through my boss. That way, I not only have the whole gang to back me up, but

I will also sidestep betrayal. Ford may not care if I shoot one of our own men in the leg, but he sure as fuck will care if I provoke a war."

Shit. I didn't think about that.

"Sorry." I mutter.

His fingers leave my throat as I step away. I walk toward the large window, taking in the beautiful scenery outside. I've come to love this house. Never in a million years would I have thought I'd sleep, let alone live, in a large mansion like this. Right now, though, I can't enjoy the view. Tears blur my vision as everything washes over me. It's all such a freaking mess. When does it stop?

Strong arms wrap around me before I'm pulled against his hard chest. Yegor buries his head against my neck as faint endearing words flow against my skin. Spinning in his arms, I slide my arms around his torso and hug him close.

"I'm sorry." I repeat. "I'm pulling you into this and…"

His head rears back and he snorts. "Sweetheart, you didn't pull me in. I was born into this shit. It's another dot on the fucking agenda. Don't trouble your pretty little head about it. Like I mentioned earlier, the marriage certificate is a statement. We need to walk a few paths to obtain our goal. Go grab a bag with a change of clothes. We'll be sleeping at Ford's house tonight because the meeting might take a few hours. You are not to be alone again. If I'm not with you, a bodyguard will be. Not just for Paco, but you're my wife now, so…"

"Lemme guess…other fucking dots on the agenda can stir shit up." I say.

And why does it bother me so much that he said the marriage certificate is a statement? A chess piece on a board, nothing more, nothing less. Laughter slips from my mouth because it's kind of ironic at this point.

Over the past weeks, I've gone through so much and so many things have crossed my path, stuff I've previously only read about in books. Some are close to the truth, others are way off. Seriously my mouth on him earlier was way more intense than any other version I've read. That makes me wonder if it will hurt more when I have sex for the first time.

"What's that thought, Ruby?" The intense look he's giving me make the words tumble from my mouth.

"Can we get the sex part over with now? I know you've created the barrier with the marriage license, but even then...something could happen." There, I need to treat it as it is...another formality, like the married part.

"No one is ever going to take you again, Ruby." His stern voice sends goosebumps all over my skin.

Ignoring the way my body reacts to him, he needs to understand where I'm coming from. "Still. I need this over and done with."

His arms leave me as he steps away from me and starts to pace the room. Anger is rolling off of him in waves. He stops midstride and snarls. "I'm not going to fuck you."

Somehow his anger triggers the same in me. "You didn't have any problems with fucking my mouth, to give me a taste, so why the hell not?" Strolling to the bed, I turn back the blanket and lay down on the virgin white bedsheets. Ironic, right? "We could snap a picture of the fresh blood and place it on social media for all to see. Send out a clear message. Bye, bye option pick-up-the-virgin-and-marry-her."

Like a predator stalking his pray, Yegor advances on me. Every time he raises his foot and place it on the ground, inching closer to me, I feel like time is on hold. The anger that was there a moment ago is nothing compared to the fury that surrounds him now. I should take my words back, but instead I decide to add more.

"Take your pleasure and I will take mine, be sure to leave some space between us so I can rub my clit." I don't know where I find the courage, but I somehow know he'd never hurt me.

Although the fierce look in his eyes would make a grown man scramble into a corner and curl into a ball, I stand firm. *Not me*. I've been through enough, and it's time to grab hold of my own life; *stand up and fight*. Something that Tarzan keeps repeating to me when she trains me. Okay, that's in self-defense, but that's what I need at this moment.

One instant I can read his emotions, and then it's gone. Standing before me is the utterly captivating, made man. Yegor has shielded me from this side of the person he really is. This must be a glimpse of what his opponents see before their time is up.

That's what's going through my mind right now. There's not a gleam in his eyes that hints at what's to come. His law, his decisions, his verdict. One thing is for sure; my time is up.

His hand inches closer, and I don't even flinch. I crave his touch. The way he took my mouth earlier? Control. That's what he had. Had. Because I for damn well know how fast he came. I remember how he was pumping his dick in his hand, a breath away from my lips.

With every pump, I was sure he would let me

wrap my lips around that thick hard length. So hot. Veins wrapped around it, the manly scent I can only link with Yegor. I was so turned on, I only needed to brush my fingers over my clit when I came at the same time his cum pumped down my throat.

"Think I would allow my wife's fingers to touch what's mine without permission?" His hand fists the fabric that covers the part between my legs. "You haven't experienced it fully yet, Ruby. How I fuck. Mouth, pussy, or ass for that matter."

His statement makes me snort. It shouldn't, but I can't help it. Does he really think he's impressing me? Throwing up statements how he has fucked all these women before me? Do I really care? Pain slices through my chest at the thought. As much as I hate to admit it, I'm jealous of those who had a part of him before me. A part that I haven't had yet. I steel myself from this weird emotion, because I can't slip, I need to focus.

Cocking one eyebrow, I shrug and pick an imaginary speck from my clothes. "Why should I care about who you fucked before me? It all involves your dick, so whip it out and start pumping. Think you can handle that much?"

Oh, shit. Did I mention earlier that I somehow know he'd never hurt me? Right…that thought just went out the window.

His grip releases on the fabric and he steps back. Without another word, Yegor leaves the room in two breaths, leaving me absolutely stunned.

CHAPTER FIVE

Stand the fuck down, Yegor.

YEGOR

I need to get a few more buddies. The kind they sell at the martial arts store. Punching bags, a sparring partner. A body opponent bag, you know what I mean...a full-sized training manikin with the upper body shaped like a human, that kinda thing. Well, you can't tell that about the shit that's piled up, or better yet, scattered all over the damned floor.

That's the fucking result of my release. My knuckles are bleeding, my knife is still lodged into the head portion of the dummy, and the gun I'm holding doesn't contain any more fucking bullets. Oh, yeah…I went all out.

Never in my whole fucking lifetime have I lost it like that. I am always in control, always. Any fucking situation I'm in, facing, or plan, I handle it with nerves of steel. And here comes this woman who can turn steel to liquid.

She's pushing every one of my buttons to rile me up. I told her I wasn't going to fuck her. I had to get out of there because I never go back on my fucking word and I almost lost control, almost. Believe me when I say I will fuck her. But not for the reasons she wants to fuck.

That shit is below me. I don't have a damn conscience, but with this? Taking her virginity because someone, my own fucking half-brother mind you, wants it for their own fucked up reasons? She needs to shake that shit because it ain't happening. Fuck no. It needs to be her decision, her longing, her fucking choice. Not a choice she's driven to.

A gasp from the doorway makes me turn. Ruby is staring at buddy. Well, what's left of buddy. Tucking my piece into my shoulder holster, I close the distance between us.

"We leave in five minutes. Like I said earlier, pack a bag." I try to step away before she can respond, but she stops my progress by wrapping her fingers around my wrist.

"You're hurt." Her voice wavers.

Glancing down at my bloody knuckles, I shrug. "Realizing shit, until you either see or feel it, doesn't mean you should fucking do something about it right away."

Her touch leaves my skin and she glares at me. "Say what you actually meant to say instead of turning that," She waves at my busted knuckles, "Into something that involves sex, or losing my virginity for that matter. That doesn't even compare except for the draw blood the first time, or feel good to blow off some build up sexual frustrations from what I'm guessing, or maybe end up sore. Hell, I don't know, because all I know is what I read or heard about it. Not that I've been living underneath a rock or something. Clearly, I've gotten off more than once using my own fingers, and…"

Oh, for fuck's sake. "Stop fucking talking about it. We need to leave; I've got shit to handle. We'll discuss this at a later point in time."

She's still glaring at me. "As long as discuss this means you'll pop my cherry in a few hours." And would you believe she actually used air quotes with her fingers to mock me? Shit.

A fucking growl rumbles deep in my throat and yet again my feet move automatically to guide me far away from her. I need more bullets for my gun and I need to place an order to get some more buddies I can fucking kill without arguments in my basement.

Finding both options in my office, I place an order while I load my gun. When I'm done, I reach inside my desk and find one of the knives I keep in there. I couldn't pull the one I'd been carrying out of the dummy's head. I always keep one on me, even if it's just a pocket knife I can open in mid-swing before I plunge it in my opponent.

My gaze lands on the pack of smokes. Strangely, I haven't craved one lately. Ever since Ruby became a part of my life, it's like I traded one addiction for another. Instead of inhaling smoke with the nicotine that sticks in my lungs, I draw her in. She's become my compulsion to continue existing. Every damn time my lungs constrict, she's the sole purpose of my reason to breathe.

"Coming?" Ruby's sweet voice floats from the doorway.

The answer 'not in your pussy any time soon' springs to mind. But I'm already tight as a…fuck… her pussy comes to mind instead of a fucking string, and I really need to fuck her to get this shit over with. I need to focus and I can't do that with my dick hard as a rock, drawing all the blood from my brain.

My only hope is that she changes her motive to fuck as soon as possible. Or at least sees my damn point of view in all of this. Fucking morals, conscience, or whatever the fucking hell that's crept its way up my ass.

Strolling over, I point in the direction of the garage. "Let's go. We're taking the Mercedes."

We don't exchange a single word during the drive to Ford's mansion. I'm fine with that little fact because I need to get my dick under control. It's like it doesn't matter whether she's sweet, normal, or feisty, one look from her and my whole body is hotwired.

That's also the reason my hand isn't on the small of her back when we step inside Ford's place. I need a little distance. With all the shit going on, I don't want to leave her side, except here it's the safest place to do so.

Tarzan comes strolling down the stairs. "Hey, do you wanna workout while the boys wrestle through a meeting?"

Deep breath in, hold it, hold it, hold it. I slowly release it, while my brain goes wild with frustrated sexual thoughts of two women going at it. See?

Everything that involves my...fuck...wife, is lighting me up. Even the thought of her sparring with my boss' wife.

"Good thinking. She can use the release." I manage to keep the groan inside my chest, while I shoot Ruby a playful wink.

Seeing I'm the one feeling tortured by all of this, I decide to return the favor. Fire shoots out of her eyes, before words wrapped with flames tumble over those plump lips I had wrapped around my cock not too long ago.

"Yes, he's right. Seeing as my husband doesn't know how to handle a woman's need. Consummating a wedding night is foreign to the idiot who tied me down in black and white. So..." Ruby's gaze shifts to Tarzan. "Care to tie me up with one of your silky ropes and do your worst?"

"Step away from my woman before I throw you out on your ass, bitch." Ford growls, and my fist connects with his jaw the moment the word bitch left his mouth.

I'm getting ready to block the fucker lashing out when Tarzan's back is in the way. Her hands are on her hips and she's laying into her husband. "That was unnecessary."

The bosses, funny little detail seeing both Ford and Tarzan are both equally in charge of the Dudnik Circle, are angry. "Ruby was only messing with Yegor. Why don't you boys go and talk so us girls can do the same?"

"You're not going to work out together anymore." Ford growls against Tarzan's face.

Tarzan shakes her head. "Not your call, boss." She throws back in a sing song voice.

Stepping around them, I see Ruby glaring at me like all of this is my damn fault. I'm heading in the direction of the meeting room when her voice freezes me mid stride.

"You could have avoided this shit, you know that, right? Instead of pumping in my mouth, you should have aimed a little lower." Her voice is harsh and loud.

"Holy shit." Ford grumbles while Tarzan mutters the same words.

Spinning on my heel, I get right in her face, our noses touching. "If you'd asked me to fuck you for any other reason than the wish to no longer be a virgin because my brother wants you for the exact same thing, we would still be at my house with my dick buried deep for the sixth time."

Ruby gasps, and a flash of guilt and understanding washes over her face. Fuck. I should have kept my big mouth shut.

"Forget what I said," I grumble and drag a hand through my hair. "I need to talk through some shit with Ford. Wait in my room; I'll be there within the hour to fuck you. I'll make sure to ask Tori to get a room ready for you, so you can sleep in there after I pop your cherry. Apparently, you won't need my services after that. Well, aside from keeping you safe before I take care of my brother." Without looking back, I stride into the conference room and slam the door shut.

I place my hands on the table to brace myself. My chest is heaving and my blood is pounding in my ears. It's the loudest damn noise ever. From the corner of my eye, I see the door open. Pushing myself off the table, I cross my arms in front of my chest.

"Stand the fuck down, Yegor." Ford mutters as he closes the door and flips the lock.

I grab a chair and drag it back before I plant my ass on it. "I don't know how the hell you handle your wife. Dammit. Ruby is driving me insane."

"Mind telling me why the fuck you guys are married all of a sudden? And why the hell is there bitching about popping cherries? In. My. Fucking. Foyer. For Christ's sake." He sounds as frustrated as I feel.

"It was Paco who placed the order to have her taken. They wanted her to know he was the one who'd rape and kill her....except...she wasn't to be touched. You know what that means, right? She's a virgin. The tradition these guys have leads me to believe he wanted to marry her." I scrub a hand down my face, suddenly feeling very tired.

"It's time for that fucking half-brother of yours to stop breathing. That's the only way to be rid of the stain that's stamped on your life. Fuck the truce the syndicate made years ago. They should never have done that shit in the first place. Keeping the peace between gangs is a priority, but..." Ford's voice trails off.

I slam my hand on the table. "Don't you think I fucking know that? If they hadn't made the deal, it would have been a fucking bloodbath on both sides." Unable to keep my cool, I start to pace through the room. "That's the fucking reason I had the marriage license drawn up. She's mine now and he needs to respect it or he'll set off a war his own people won't support."

Ford nods. "Yeah, damn smart move on your part. It buys us time to plot his murder."

"Fuck, yes." I agree, and that's the reason we work so damn well together. Always on the same wave length, like we share a brain.

"Any idea's how you want to handle this?" He folds his hands in front of him.

I know he's already making plans in his head, but I've been at it longer and with Ford asking me first, he's clearly letting me assume the lead. "We set up a meeting. I need to look the fucker in the eye to make it clear he's going down."

Ford's mouth flattens to a thin line while he shakes his head. "No. Instead of a meeting, we host a party. Our turf. We feel the fucker out, because I've heard they've touched base with another Italian gang."

"Ricca 'The Fox' Dantano." I throw out the name of the head of the gang he's referring to.

I heard that rumor a while ago too. I've avoided my half-brother for years, but I always keep tabs on him. I need to be in the know about what's going on. You can't afford to be caught off guard. Not with these guys. Not in my profession…hell, not in my life.

"I'll make sure to invite that fucker too. I'm in the mood to spice things up." Ford chuckles.

That thought makes me snort. "Then by all means, invite Peacock. I'm sure he wouldn't miss it for the world."

Peacock is the leader of another gang. We're in good standing with this one, a loyal friend and partner when we team up. Occasionally, we have to handle big shit that requires safety in numbers and you always want someone to have your back.

"I'll get our computer nerds to do another round of full background checks. Because,"

I cut Ford off. "Smart, who knows what changed the last time I checked the fucker. Let them dig into The Fox too. I don't want any surprises."

Ford takes out his phone and shoots off a message.

"Right, well…I'll set another meeting for tomorrow. That will give the triple A nerd team enough time to heat up their computers and give us some intel. Now, I heard you have a wife to…uhmmm, deflower and shit." Ford's laughter fills the room and I really should be angry but I can't help but join in.

Rubbing both of my hands over my face, I mutter, "Fuck, she's more than a fucking handful. I shouldn't be having these damn moral issues. I've bathed in blood and somehow I struggle to fuck my own goddamn wife."

"When it kills you on that level, it only shows how deeply she's already wormed inside you. Embrace it, sucker. I did." Ford turns and heads for the door. "Now I'm going to go find my woman. She's got some punishment coming her way, first my hand on her ass and then she'll get to deal with my dick."

Stalking to the door, I follow him to the gym room, because I need to do the same thing.

CHAPTER SIX

It sucks to have problems.

Ruby

"Then you jump and kick the fucker in the chest, but then you gotta brace for the fall, like this." Tarzan runs at the fake dude we use to practice fight moves with and kicks it with both feet before she goes down. Within a blink of an eye, she's back on her feet.

"Wow. Yeah, I'd be doing a head dive after that and get knocked out the second I hit the floor." I shake my head, because clearly, that's way out of my league.

Tarzan releases a deep sigh. "But you know what you can do when you're on the ground, right?"

"Kick upward, hit his dick, or aim for the knee. Bring him down. I know." I nod furiously, because I'm loving the things she has drilled into my brain.

She graces me with an approving smile. "Good. Okay, what next? You wanna go back to the palm straight up the nose?"

I return the smile. "Ooooh, come on and show me again. Please. That totally kicks ass when you do that. You move your hands so fast it's like watching a windmill during a tornado."

Tarzan can do this flat hand, knuckle, elbow combination thing with the dummy's face so it appears as a blur of punches she literally rains down. It was one of the first things she taught me. I know how to do it, except mine is definitely a slow-motion version of hers.

She rolls her eyes and strolls to the wall on my left where her bag sits. Tarzan reaches inside and takes out a knife. As she stalks toward me,

I'm immediately on edge. Instead of fear, she taught me to see and think. Keep your head clear and let your body react how it's been trained. So I do.

"Dammit, Tarzan, put the fucking knife down." Yegor growls from behind me.

Even his voice doesn't distract me as Tarzan lunges straight at me, the knife pointed in my direction. I easily sidestep and come up behind her. I grab her face with my hands while I lace my fingers and throw her backwards on the ground, placing my boot on her wrist that's holding the knife.

Tarzan's laughter fills the room while I jump up and down and clap my hands. Yeah, total girly reaction, but it was the first time I did it right from the start. Normally, she'd use an unloaded gun; this is the first time she used a sharp object.

"This ends now. You make sure your woman knows I'm taking over this part. Throw that stuff in with the punishment or some shit." Yegor says to Ford before he grabs me by the arm. He swings me up and I am suddenly looking at the world from an upside-down point of view because he's carrying me out of the room, fireman style.

"Put me down right now." I don't even know if I should be angry, laugh, or go crazy.

He's been a bouncing ball of emotions, wanting me and then pushing me away at the next turn. With everything that he does that involves me. I find it very hard to get a read on him.

I mean, he put his dick in my mouth and clearly wants me. Hell, he married me. Yet he mentioned the marriage certificate as a matter of fact, not something done out of love, the way it should be. Then he voiced his morals, shocking me.

All of this makes me realize that I pulled him into this, and I haven't thought about his feelings. All I have cared about is revenge, and I've been using everything within reach to get it. Including Yegor. He's done enough already, and I need to step back because apparently, I'm a selfish bitch.

"I need to pee. Put me down or I'm gonna wet my pants." There. I'm actually pissed at myself so that's the reason I threw that out.

He freaking chuckles. "That's a lie, Ruby."

"Wanna bet? Because I'm mentally counting how many clean pairs of pants I have so I can pee right now to prove my point, or piss…whatever." I grumble.

I yelp in surprise when he smacks my ass.

"Go on and pee, woman. I don't fucking care. I've gotten dirty in a lot more ways, so getting peed on won't ever stop me from taking care of business." His voice is stern, yet casual.

It slices straight through my heart and makes me go limp. When we reach a room upstairs, Yegor closes the door behind us and slides me down his body to place me on my feet. I immediately step away from him.

Yegor doesn't even glance in my direction as he strolls to the bed and tosses back the covers. He grips the hem of his shirt and peels it over his head, dropping it to the ground. His hands reach for his belt.

"Stop." I say.

I don't even recognize my own voice. That single word slices hard through the silence the room has wrapped us in. He turns slowly and pins me with a gaze that prompt me to step back. His eyes are dark, eyebrows drawn down as his head slowly tilts to the left. His shoulders are thrown back, his upper body sculpted in a fierce armor of muscles and ink.

I need to swallow before I can manage to push words out of my mouth. "I don't want this."

A sly smile tugs his lips before his features shift to feral. "Yes. You do. Ass on the bed, Ruby. *Now*."

I try to scoot away a little further, only to find my back is already against the wall. With my next breath, Yegor has me midair, and then I'm landing on the mattress. Bouncing, I reach out and fist the bedsheets.

"Next time I ask you to do something, do it. I won't ask twice, and you'll find out what the consequences will be. I should add you won't like them, so fucking listen." His voice is cold. No emotion. Except for his eyes, which are flaming, daring me to challenge him.

I know he's a made man. Hard, a killer, always in control. Maybe I should fear him too. Like my first instinct was the second he put me down in this room. Except…I can't. All I've done is push him, use him, and fight him. Never once did I place him first or even think about what this all entails for him. I am the epitome of selfish.

Scrambling to my feet, I stand on the bed and poke my finger against his chest. "No."

"No?" His eyebrows reach for the ceiling and his hands ball into fists at his sides.

Okay, big girl panties, I've got them and they are huge, yet snug…I can do this. "You heard me. I said no. You put your ass on the bed. Right now."

The corner of his mouth turns up while he slowly shakes his head. "Never gonna happen, gorgeous."

Right when I'm about to give a snarky reply, a loud bang comes from the adjacent room. Yegor reaches for his gun and races for the door. Without thinking, I run after him. He shoves the door open and aims his gun.

I place a hand on his back to let him know I'm right behind him. His arm swings back and he pushes me to the side so I'm completely shielded by his large body. I can't help but stand on my toes to take a peek over his shoulder. Apparently, our caution is unnecessary, because Yegor tucks away his gun and shakes his head.

"Fucking lover's quarrel, minus the lovers. They should just confess their love and screw each other's brains out." He mutters to himself.

Peeking around him, I see Tori, Nathan's sister, standing with her arms crossed in front of her chest and a smirk painted on her face. Clearly, she's not impressed by the man standing in front of Yegor. All I can see is his back, but I know it's Borya.

From what I noticed before I left to live in Yegor's mansion, and from what I've been told by both Nathan and Tarzan, these two are like fire and ice. I have no idea what he's saying because Borya is deaf and he speaks in American Sign Language. His arms are waving in front of him while his hands frantically sign.

My gaze shifts to the right and I see a large dresser lying on the floor. That must be what caused the loud noise.

Yegor turns around. "Come on, leave them to it."

His fingers wrap around my upper arm and he guides me out of the room.

I'm still peering over my shoulder. "You sure they're gonna be okay?"

Yegor closes the door behind me and flips the lock. "Yeah, I happen to know Afon took Tori out yesterday. Or at least, he made it look like that. But it wasn't. It's a going in circles kinda thing where Borya needs to wake the hell up and take what he wants. Tori isn't going to wait forever. Hell, between the two of them, she quit just as many times as he fired her. She was hired as his nurse to look after him because he was burned in a car bomb. But he's healing nicely and there won't be anything else to keep her here. He's clearly in love with the chick, but he won't claim her or leave her. Fucking idiot. Honesty is the key if you want to pursue something you crave in life. Mainly to yourself. Or you're bound to let it slip from your fingers."

"Are you still talking about Borya and Tori, or are you trying to tell me something here?" I mutter, because…

"What's that, Ruby? Hear something that hits a little close to home?" A satisfied grin spreads across those sinful lips of his.

Ugh. I really want to smack it right off.

"I'm sorry, okay? I'm selfish. But you know what? It sucks to have problems I can't handle alone. I'm aware of what I'm asking of you, of how I pulled you into my shit. It wasn't like I held my nose, closed my eyes and took a dip. I was pulled into this shit and didn't have a choice. Okay…I did. And I choose you." Shit. That last sentence sounded more like an admission to myself than to him.

Yegor slightly shakes his head. "Right. But for what reason, eh?"

"The right one." I snap.

"I'm tired. I'm going to hit the shower and crash."

He doesn't even look at me but stalks off to the bathroom. *What the hell?*

"Don't you dare walk away from me. I was talking to you." I seethe while I chase him into the bathroom.

He arches one eyebrow. "You call that talking?"

His hands reach for his waist and before I know what's happening, I'm staring at one hell of a large penis. Dick....shit. Cock. Large. Thick. Hard. With veins wrapped around it and a hand tugging and it's mesmerizing. Shit.

Spinning around, I close my eyes and slap my hands over my face. Even though it's unnecessary, considering my back is blocking the view, the vision is now burned into my brain and I can't shake the image.

The water is turned on, just as freely as I am, and that makes me slowly spin around. Just in time to see one hard and nicely shaped ass stepping underneath the shower.

At this point I've got nothing to lose. I feel like Yegor has slipped away from me. "I've never had a boyfriend, or even a guy friend. None of this is easy, and I'm sorry I hurt your feelings or made you feel like I'm only using you. Hell, I know I am. But I was ripped away from my home, stolen from my own life. You brought me back, but I still had nothing. Then you wrecked me. You. A person I didn't know and yet with the sound of your voice, I instinctively knew you and only you would keep me safe. I'm messed up. Seriously." I take a deep breath and swallow the huge lump in my throat. Damn these feelings. My gaze inspects the tiles I'm standing on. "I'm truly sorry if I make you feel like I'm using you. Some people are fit to handle whatever needs to be done. I'm sorry I didn't see you as a person. For that I am...truly sorry. Because if there's one person on this earth I feel connected to on more than one level...it's you."

I feel an arm wrap around me tightly before warm water pours down on me. Yegor's lips crash against mine as he pushes me against the wall. His hand is buried in my hair, keeping my head pinned against the tiles. I have no other option than to be devoured, or let's call it; Yegor possessing my mouth.

The kiss takes all the air straight from my lungs, and yet I couldn't care less. It's not the air my body needs to survive; it's the person who's making my body able to breathe him in. The sharp bite from his grip keeps me in place, while his other hand tugs down my pants. I can feel how he places his foot in the crotch of my pants and slides them down, making me step out, while his fingers dig into my left thigh.

My nails trail down his back. "I...Yegor, please."

The pressure that's building inside me is overwhelming. I have no idea what I want but I know I need something, anything.

"Please." I beg into his mouth again.

Yegor growls as he hoists me up and I wrap my legs around him. There's only an instant where I feel the tip of his dick nudging against my entrance before he pushes forward.

My scream echoes against the walls as my head falls against his shoulder. My teeth dig into his skin so I'm prevented from squealing out my pain.

Dammit, this hurts so freaking bad. It's too much. He's too much. It's like I'm being ripped open and...

"Breathe, gorgeous. Give it a moment. It will fade, and when it does...only pleasure. I promise you, love. Only pleasure." He's holding me tight, not moving, letting my body adjust to his intrusion.

Gradually, I feel the burning start to fade. My teeth release Yegor's skin and I can't help but lick the part I was holding hostage with my mouth. He groans and starts to gently move his hips. Oh. That's an immense feeling that slowly builds up. With every slide he either pulls out or fills me up, and it builds fire inside my veins.

I'm gasping for air while I struggle to bring his body closer to mine. Except...there's no space left between us. We're connected, mind, body, and soul, when my insides explode into pure bliss that's so overwhelming it feels as though time stops.

Yegor grunts against my neck where his head is buried while his hips keep pumping. Hot pulsing strokes inside me, branding me while it fuels the euphoria in both our bodies.

"Damn." Yegor grumbles between breaths.

I can only manage a slight nod of my head in agreement.

"Rhapsody. First fuck. Your pussy was made to take my cock." I feel his words rumble from his chest before they stroke my ears.

I pull back and look in his eyes, only to find him pinning me with an intense gaze, daring me to disagree.

I feel a smile spreading over my face, while my eyes drop to his lips. "You're mistaken."

A snarl leaves his mouth, making me chuckle.

"Because I know for a fact it's your cock that was made for my pussy." Sounds the same, right? Yeah, no. The difference is submission. My pussy is clearly superior.

"Whatever, Ruby. It's mine." He takes away my chance to form words by covering his mouth with mine.

Doesn't matter…obviously, it's a win-win for both of us.

CHAPTER SEVEN

Maybe there are more to kill.

YEGOR

I'm staring down at Ruby's angelic face, basking in the fact she is sleeping in my bed without a care in the world. Just like the content feeling that's rooted deep in my heart. The bumpy ride that led to this moment is something I will value and draw energy from. Especially because I know there will be lots more of that shit coming our way.

I breathe in a few more moments with her before I meander away and close the door behind me.

I take my time descending the stairs to the meeting Ford requested. He wants us to meet in the living room along with Afon and Borya. Yeah, this should be nice and cozy with those two fuckers in the same space.

They need to put their differences aside, and let's hope they do, because there are more important things going on right now. Like killing my brother. Not to mention, we are having the party before the actual act. Funny, because Paco doesn't know he's the guest of honor. It's presumptuous to celebrate his death prematurely, but I'm totally good with that. Because one way or the other, he is going to die.

"Congratulations are in order, I hear." Afon slaps me on the back.

Smiling proudly, I say, "That's right. My wife is sleeping upstairs."

"Took you long enough to tie that one to you. Happy to know you finally managed to get it done. So, what is this other thing?" Afon rubs his hands together gleefully. "We get to host a party and kill people? Fun times."

Borya enters the room and smacks Afon upside the back of the head, he signs as we both pin our eyes to his hands. Being deaf doesn't hold him back at all. He uses American Sign Language to communicate and can lip read as well, which can be handy in certain situations. Ford made sure that all of us learned the basics of ASL so communication is possible. As long as the man isn't giving a dissertation I can usually follow along. "We're only going to take Paco Hurtado out. He's the one who slipped through the cracks during the snuff movie wrap up."

Ford strolls into the room with Tarzan behind him.

"Have a seat." Ford points to the two couches that are positioned across from each other.

Tarzan plants her ass on a cushion and immediately bounces back and glares at Ford. Damn. I so don't need to know about her ass being red and burning from the spanking she got. Hell, from the one I requested that my boss give her because I didn't like her interfering with my woman. Yes, I know she did an awesome job with training my wife, but like I told Ford…that's my job from now on.

Ford grabs Tarzan by her waist and drags her onto his lap. "I called you guys because I've been in contact with Peacock. He told me that Paco has been bumping heads with Ricca 'The Fox' Dantano. From the outside, it might seem like they are walking hand in hand, but the reality is that Paco wants to incorporate The Fox's gang into his. The Fox can't point to any physical proof, but he knows Paco is behind some personal as well as business failures. The Fox gladly accepted our invitation and is looking forward to the party. Needless to say, so is Peacock. He's also bringing his wife."

Tarzan glows with excitement. "She's badass. One of the best hitmen, or should I say hitwomen? Fuck, assassins, out there."

"Why are all of the woman kicking ass all of a sudden?" I grumble, because fuck…I know it's kinda badass that they can defend themselves and shit, but it's kinda intimidating and unsettling at the same time.

"I need to get me one of those." Afon chimes in.

Borya stands up, walks over to Afon and smacks him on the head...again.

Afon jumps up and pushes Borya in the chest, causing him to step back and brace himself. "Try it again, fucker. I'll kick your ass."

"You find your own woman. Stay the hell away from mine." Borya signs.

Afon throws his shoulders back. "Aw, come on now...learn to share, she's..."

"Afon." Tarzan snaps.

He ducks the punch Borya throws at his chin, and then holds his hands up in front of him. "All right, all right. I'm only screwing with your head, Borya. I have no plans for your lady. But you need to tell her that she's yours. For real, put a ring on her finger already, because you'll lose her if you don't. For fuck's sake, man the hell up."

"Can we stick to my fucking problems right now? Because my woman is lying in my bed, naked I might add, and I'm standing here listening to fucking schoolboys going at it." I growl out my frustration.

Afon turns. "Ah, yes…let's discuss your woman, because that went well."

"Afon." Tarzan cracks out again

"Fine." Afon snaps and heads for the door. "I'll be going now. Text me the details if there's something I should know. All of you idiots have something to put your dick in. I'm off to find something warm and tight to wrap around mine."

"Use your hand later, idiot. Now sit the fuck down because I wasn't done talking," Ford bellows. "I've got some information about The Fox. He's been known to organize high roller cruises, and the…"

"Dammit." Another few curses leave my mouth. All eyes are on me when I start to pace the room. "Ruby's friend took this job as a waitress on classy cruises. The night they were taken, she asked Ruby to help her out and come along. The snuff movie fuckers snatched them up the second they stepped foot on that fucking ship."

"So it could have been this Fox guy that had her taken instead of Paco?" Tarzan asks.

I rub a hand over my mouth while I think things over. "Could be. Or Paco tried to pin him with the murder or tried to pull something else. Maybe he didn't want to marry Ruby because she was a virgin. Or something entirely different is going on."

Ford's voice catches our attention. "We need Ruby here to talk things through. Does she know Paco, or hell, The Fox, anything? If so we need to know."

He's right. "I'll go get her."

I take the stairs two at a time and it only builds my anger. I know she told me some, but I sure as hell know my boss will lob question after question at her. We need to know every detail. Even if it's the brand of shoes she was wearing or a fucking speck on her shirt...we need to know.

I swing the door open, and my gaze fixes on the bed. Shock slides through my veins when I see it's empty. Scanning the room, I come up with no trace of her. *Where the hell is she?* Suddenly, I see a tiny shred of red peeking from behind the bedside table.

Rounding the bed, I see Ruby huddled against the wall, her knees drawn up to her chest. Her eyes fly open and a look of sheer panic floods her face. I can't help but fall to my fucking knees and pull her against me. Her fists wrap around the fabric of my shirt as she tries to drag me even closer.

"You scared me." Her words are muffled against my chest.

I scared her? "Gorgeous, why aren't you sleeping in the bed?"

She ignores my question and seems to brace herself because she's pulling away from me. "I have to pee."

Yeah, right. "You can't use that line with me, Ruby. I can see right through that shit."

"Not shit, I said pee." She laughs, and it's like she has to make a fucking effort to make it sound like actual laughter.

"No one is ever going to take you again, Ruby. I promise you now and forever. I will be right here by your side, and I will fight or kill every single person who dares to try and harm you." The vow is just as much for her as it is for me.

She stands up and smooths out the shirt she's wearing. "Right, well…I'm gonna, go…uhm."

"You need to come with me downstairs. We're talking things through and something came up, we need you to tell us your story so we're not missing anything." As soon as I've said those words, I see fear in her eyes right before she pushes it way and nods.

"Okay, lemme throw on some pants." She replies absently while she reaches for her bag and pulls out a dark green yoga pants.

After putting them on, Ruby takes out a large gray sweatshirt and throws it over the shirt she was sleeping in. Right next to the fucking bed. On. The. Ground. Sitting up for crying out loud. My heart breaks when I realize no one was there for her after her ordeal. And then here I come and demand she cut Nathan and Tarzan out of the picture.

Dammit, I'm an asshole.

When we walk to the living room, I sit on the couch and make sure Ruby sits next to me so I can tuck her underneath my arm. From now on, I'll be the one she can lean on, but first.

"Tarzan." My boss' head snaps my way when she hears her name.

I let out a heavy breath because in one way, this will be easy...but in another way, I'm going to hear about my dick getting soft from my other boss.

"I'd like to make sure you'll still teach Ruby how to fight. I'll train her too, but...yeah. You should..." I clear my throat, because that's all I have right now.

Tarzan's eyes widen before her head flashes to Ford. It's as if she needs his permission or some... shit... In a way she does; I made him punish her for it. See? Yeah. But when I look down and feel Ruby's hand lean on my thigh, while she pushes herself up to give me a soft kiss on my cheek. The *thank you* that flows from her mouth might as well hotwire my dick, because he's trying to wave *you're welcome* at her from behind the zipper.

"We should really have a new rule that allows us to have dude meetings without estrogen present." Afon mutters.

"Careful now." Tarzan snaps.

"Sorry, Boss." Afon replies.

I'm pretty sure his attitude is piled up frustration because his dick isn't getting any action.

Tarzan leans forward and puts her elbows on her knees. "We were going to continue our sessions anyway. Right, Ruby?" She doesn't give my wife time to agree before she lays out the situation. "We need you to tell us exactly what happened the day you were taken. Start with the time you woke up and don't spare any details. Even if you think it's nothing, it might trigger something that can lead to more information. Okay?"

Ruby nods and starts to relay the memories she already told me, about her friend and what she remembers from that night. Everyone else in the room is quiet until she finishes with the words, "And then everything went dark."

"You were drugged. What do you remember after you woke up? Were you on that bed where we found you? Do you remember anything else?" Tarzan's voice is gentle.

"I woke up because Ava was shaking me. The moment my eyes flew open, I threw up. God, I was so sick, and I couldn't comprehend what was happening. Ava kept shaking me, telling me to wake up and get on my feet, but I couldn't. We were on the floor, in a room with steel walls. No windows, just a door. There was a tiny bed in the corner and a desk in the middle of the room. When I finally was able to get on my feet, the door flew open and three men stepped inside."

Every muscle in my body goes rigid. This part is all new to me. She only shared the part how she ended up with that snuff movie making gang, how they snatched her from that cruise...not what the fuck happened afterward. I bite the inside of my cheek, because I don't know if I'm ready to hear this shit. And she went through it.

Her hand on my thigh tightens, and I cover it with my own, lacing her fingers with mine.

Somehow she feeds on my support to continue. "Two of them grabbed me and kept me in place while the other dragged Ava to the desk. He...he..."

Aw, fuck. "They raped and killed Ava right in front of Ruby, made her fucking watch."

There. That part needs to be skipped because it cuts straight through my heart and I don't even have the images branded on my brain like Ruby does.

"Yes." Ruby's voice trembles. "They did. While they all kept saying; He's coming for you. Paco Hurtado wants to fuck your cunt and slice your neck."

"They said he wanted to fuck and kill you? Those exact words?" Ford asks.

Ruby nods. "Yes. That's the same line they kept repeating to me."

"You weren't to be touched at all because Paco wanted to fuck you himself and then kill you. That's..." Ford locks eyes with mine. "Not wanted to marry her then?"

I shrug. "Could have been a trick to scare the shit out of her and mold her into agreeing to anything. Who knows? Maybe it's an order of business? Paco and The Fox...the fucker might have set it up to rip away the option for The Fox to fuck her." Hell. "Or rape and kill her and then throw her on the fucker's doorstep."

"Who? What are you talking about? What do you guys know?" Ruby is bouncing her gaze back and forth between me and Ford.

Turning my body slightly toward her, I make sure her eyes meet mine. "Do you know about a guy named Ricca Dantano? They also call him The Fox."

"The Fox? For real? That's just weird. And no, I haven't heard of anyone by that name." Ruby shakes her head.

"Were you dating anyone at the time?" Tarzan asks. "Someone who you ran into? Had an eye on you maybe? Did you receive any gifts or flowers, or did anything unusual happen in the days leading up to when you were kidnapped?"

Damn, Tarzan is good.

Again, I find myself chewing the side of my cheek because bright green jealousy is running through me. Something I've never encountered before and it's about shit that happened before I even met her.

"No boyfriend, no flowers or," Ruby's eyebrows lower as though she's thinking things over.

"What's that thought, Ruby? Let us know, even if you think it's nothing. Don't mind your husband next to you looking all ferocious and ready to start dismembering bodies. It happened in the past, so don't worry." Tarzan chuckles.

Ruby's gaze meets mine, I try like hell to school my features but clearly, I fail.

Her fingertips brush my cheek and my woman shoots me a cheeky grin before she leans in and whispers, "That's a very sexy look."

The clearing of a throat reminds me there are other people in the room and by the way Ruby's cheeks flush, I'm sure she forgot too.

"Right," she said. "Well, there was this guy about a week before it happened…I worked as a secretary at a car dealership. He came,"

"Where? What kind of cars? Name? Was it a family business?" Afon is holding his iPad and is waiting for her to answer his questions.

I'm sure it's because he wants to dig in, or get the info to our computer nerds who can dig in deeper.

"Sports Car Valley. They sell,"

"Ferrari's." I finish for her, because yeah…I know the company. "It's a family business. Hamm, an older couple."

Ruby nods. "I'd worked for them for about two weeks when I realized their son is a total asshole. He made it clear I should reveal a nice amount of cleavage because that holds the client's attention." Ruby's clenching my hand in a death grip.

"What happened, Ruby?" I manage to keep some of the bite from my tone.

She tenses, and I squeeze her fingers gently, encouraging her to continue. "Like I said, there was a guy who came in and he was interested in buying a Ferrari. I was working a half day, I was leaving and was outside when I realized I forgot my purse. So I went back in and leaned over the desk to grab my purse and,"

I can't help but groan. "Ruby. Bending over? Really?"

She rolls her eyes. "Hey, that's a huge freaking desk we're talking about. Bending over instead of going around was saving me at least a minute or two. Anyway…when I turned with my purse in hand, that asshole son of theirs tapped a client against the chest and sneered; 'What did I tell you? That's a nice piece of ass. I can probably get her to spread her legs for you,'"

I'm off the couch, gripping my hair with two hands. "He's dead. I'm heading over right now."

Ruby gasps behind me when I pull out my gun and double check to make sure it's loaded.

"Sit your ass down, Yegor." Tarzan waves a hand toward the couch. "Wait till you hear the rest. For all you know, there are more bodies to add to our kill count, and I can come with you to share in the fun."

Fuck, she's right. It would be a shame to have to go back to kill some more. "Go on, Ruby."

She closes her eyes with a little shake of her head. Clearly disapproving, and yet there's a smile painted on those lovely lush lips.

CHAPTER EIGHT

Any chance of a double orgasm?

Ruby

Something must be wrong with me, because who in their right mind thinks it's hot when their husband wants to kill a man who only spoke a few nasty words about me?

"Go on, Ruby." Yegor presses.

I debate pulling my knees up to hide my face, because I feel a smile tugging at my lips. Dammit. Okay, focus, I can do this.

My gaze connects with Tarzan because that

makes the words flow easier. "So the douchebag throws that out and before I can blink, the man he was talking to wraps his fingers around douchebag's throat. He told him to apologize, to get down on his knees, because that was no way to talk to a lady. That right there didn't make me popular, although the guy did buy a Ferrari but he told the douchebag that he only bought it because he enjoyed seeing me, a lovely woman who brightened his day."

"So glad I stayed. Lemme have this fucker's name, because I need to track him down too." Yegor growls.

I shake my head. "Oh, no you don't. He was a nice guy. I told him that I wasn't interested in a relationship or dating. He wanted to go out and sent me flowers the next day. He was…"

"Feel free to either shut the fuck up or gimme the goddamn name." This time Yegor bellows out his words.

I cross my arms in front of my chest. "Oh, shut it. He was the only guy in my life who was really sweet to me. And I,"

"Shush, Ruby. Don't feed the beast beside you; it's like the hulk. Anger builds his muscles and the green is all on the inside. Did you ever see this nice guy again? Remember his name? Anything?" Tarzan asks.

Her words prompt me to gasp. "No way am I telling you his name." I point a finger at Yegor. "If I do, you'll dash off and kill him."

"Yeah, well, there's that." Tarzan shrugs. "Or we might find out Paco used one of his aliases and met you for the first time that day. It would explain a lot."

I could smack myself upside the head. "Nooooo. Damn. You're smart. He said his name was Riccardo."

"Ricca." Yegor curses.

Ford adds a few curses of his own. "It would be something. They were getting along at that time. Ricca could have mentioned something to Paco. Maybe things went sour after that and Paco thought it would be fun to chuck a dead girl Ricca's way to make the point he's always in charge. By taking the girl Ricca tried to impress, they can tie it back to him."

Wait, what? "So this Ricca placed a huge bulls-eye on my head. What the hell?"

I stalk to Yegor and hold out my hand. "Gun."

I wiggle my fingers while I keep a steady palm up, indicating that I want him to hurry the hell up and give it to me. He smiles wickedly and reaches back, pulls his gun from his holster, but right before he can place it in my hand, Ford's voice cuts through the air.

"Put it away, Yegor. You know damn well if this theory is true, you'll have one hell of an ally in Ricca." Dammit. Even to me that's logical and my hands drop.

I can't help but stomp my foot and mutter underneath my breath. "Dammit. I really looked forward to…"

I don't get to finish my sentence because I need to bite my tongue to prevent from moaning. Yegor's lips are on my skin where the curve of my neck meets my collarbone.

"Patience adds to the intense pleasure that washes over you when the moment is finally there."

His breath is so close to me it ignites a shiver that sends goosebumps over my skin.

"Hmmm. That's why you wanted to jump the gun and hightail it out of here a few times, right?"

"Gorgeous, I have no need for patience. I'm the epitome of living in the present."

His words make me snort. "Mister Right Now, I presume?"

"Okay, yikes. You two head up and get some 'Right Now' action, while the big boys start planning shit." Afon mutters while he shoos us away with both hands.

Yegor doesn't even argue. He spins me around and places his hand at the small of my back to guide me out of the room. But instead of leading me up the stairs, he takes a detour. We descend stairs and we're now underneath the mansion. There are all different kinds of rooms left and right, but he leads me all the way back. As soon as we step inside a room, I clearly see what it is. An indoor shooting range. *Nice.*

Yegor makes a beeline to a rack in the back

and grabs a couple guns and boxes of ammo. "Ever shoot a gun before, Ruby?"

"Nope. But I gather that's about to change, right?" I can't hide the anticipation in my voice.

"Yeah, gorgeous. We're gonna do some damage." He sets down the gun and starts to load the magazine. When he's done, his gaze hits mine. "Crank the magazine in here." His palm hits the butt of the gun before his hand moves to the top. "Then slide this back so there's a round in the chamber. Now you want a firm grip, like this. Two hands, Ruby, don't get all wild west on me and wave it around. Also, what I showed you with the slide? That part moves each time so keep your hand clear from that, yes?" He waits for me to nod before he continues. "Two hands straight forward. Because if you hold it like a pansy, it will wiggle around or fly out of your hand."

"Like a pansy." A gush of air leaves my mouth. "As if. I know how to hold on to something."

I'm fairly annoyed by his words, because I remember all too well how he didn't even want my hands around his dick. When his eyes narrow, I know he's thinking about the same thing. He sets the gun on a shelf, and within seconds his fingers wrap around my neck and he walks me back against the wall.

His thumb slides up and feathers across my bottom lip. "Let's get one thing very clear, Ruby. You're mine. You might think that gives you some control, but that's an utter illusion. Whether you're naked or standing fully clothed in the middle of a theme park, I own you. Every inch that is you and every way you take my dick. Even when it's barely an inch of my dick I decide to slide between those delectable lips. Everything is something I own. Mine. Got it?"

"Yegor's bitch. Got it." I snap.

There's a low rumble emanating from his chest. His eyes darken and his fingers tighten slightly around my neck.

"It rubs me the wrong way, okay?" I growl right back, annoyed because I feel the need to explain while he's the one acting all caveman.

131

"I mean, if you were rubbing my clit while throwing out Neanderthal statements, then maybe I'd consider it sexy."

I feel his hand sliding in my waistband and a little scream leaves my lips. "Damn, cold fingers."

Icicles. His finger is like an icicle rubbing my clit. But it's spreading heat through my whole body, dragging a moan from me that I was trying very hard to keep inside.

"Ruby." He says my name in a way that commands an answer, but I only manage a groan in response.

"Who are you?" He drawls while he takes my clit between two fingers, keeping it hostage while he shoots out his demands.

"Yours, I'm yours." I rush out the words because I need to draw air into my lungs for the orgasm that rips through me.

"That's right. And don't fucking forget it. I might overlook you replying with Yegor's bitch, but that's only if you come for me beautifully the next instant to drag my attention away. Because I don't fucking condone you being referred to as bitch, even when you're the one saying it. Clear?" His tongue slides from my earlobe to my chin, where he nips my skin. "Clear?"

Oh, reply. Shit. His fingers sliding through my pussy are such a distraction. "Yegor's bitch, right."

A sharp sting spreads between my legs before his hand is gone. Did he just smack my pussy?

Yegor's arms are crossed in front of his chest while he glares at me and slowly shakes his head. "Now, Ruby, another thing I do not condone is manipulation. I want your hands on the shelf and push that tight ass back for me."

My mouth goes dry and it's hard to swallow. The fierce look in his eyes doesn't leave any room for argument. I drag my feet all the way toward the shelf.

"I didn't mean to, dammit, but your fingers were on my clit, and you clearly said something about *Yegor's bitch* and *come the next instant*." I mutter underneath my breath.

His fingers are sliding into my hair as he tightens them into a fist. "Second time, Ruby."

"Well, since you're counting...any chance of a double orgasm then?" I might as well toss that out to piss him off some more, because I'm messing up every step I take anyway.

His hand untangles from my hair. Minutes pass... nothing's happening. I'm in place, exactly how he wanted me and nothing happens. There's no sound other than my own heart beating frantically in my ears. I'm bracing for his hand to heat up my ass, except...nothing.

Risking a glance over my shoulder, I lock eyes with Yegor. His arms are yet again crossed in front of his muscular chest. I know that underneath his white button-down shirt is some heavy ink and it just adds to the intensity he emits. His legs are slightly spread and his shoulders are tipped back as if he's bracing himself.

The only thing that looks out of place is the dark look in his eyes. And when I say out of place, I'm talking about the fact that for a person who's about to get a taste of Yegor's action…a bullet through the head, knife lodged under the chin, whatever…it's that dark look that I know it's there for me.

It's a promise, a blazing heat that comes with the desire to fuck me raw, and it's all building up and locked on the inside. Utterly calm on the outside, with a lust-filled craziness on the inside begging his inner demeanor to break lose.

It's then I realize what Nathan and Tarzan had been telling me all along. I can now see it for what it is; Mr. Inaccessible is an open book for me, and only me.

Turning, I fully face him. "For a woman who has been kidnapped, drugged, almost raped and killed… I can't help the loss and hurt that's going through my mind right now. But I don't want to change anything that got me to this point in time. If I did, I never would have met you and I never would have experienced the way you make my body come alive. Hell, you're not even touching me, just standing there, staring, making my chest burn and my heart squeeze. I might seem like I've lost my mind or don't recognize the person I am anymore. This whole marriage certificate might be meant as a statement, but you've made it clear...that's all it is. I tried, but I fail to see it that way. I might as well be in there fully because I don't do things with half a brain, I tend to go all in. You ask; who are you? There's only one thing my body and mind scream in sync...I'm yours; Yegor's woman." I just threw my heart at him, leaving me to hold my breath, because there's no change in his body language.

Unease fills me. "I'm not trying to manipulate you into giving me an orgasm, dammit."

The single movement of the left side of his mouth coming up in a satisfied grin is an indication my words didn't leave him cold. "Turn that ass around; hands on the shelf, Ruby."

Hurt slams into me by the lack of emotion in his voice. I mean, I did throw my heart out to him...did he catch it? No. More like hit the pause button so he could order takeout and hit play when it suits him.

"Fine. Have it your way." I mutter while I turn and manage to swallow some curses that threaten to spill from the hurt that's filling my veins.

My fingers curl around the shelf where the loaded gun is laying on top. Without a sound, I feel Yegor molding his body to mine, one hand snakes over my hip, up my belly and finds my right breast. He pinches the nipple through the fabric while his other hand covers my pussy possessively.

His mouth is right next to my ear. "I'll always have my way, best to remember that."

Shit, I'm so screwed. I suck at remembering things when his hand is on my pussy.

CHAPTER NINE

The trigger, not my dick.

YEGOR

I'm not trying to manipulate you. Her words echo in my brain. Hell, if she could read my mind I'd be a lost cause for the simple reason I don't need any manipulation when it comes to her. All she has to do is ask and I'd drop to my knees and kiss the fucking ground she walks on.

That's right. It takes every cell in my body to keep my cool. She has no clue what she does to me. Laying her heart out like that… saying the actual words that I've wanted to hear from the moment I saw her…fuck. My emotions are running wild.

But instead of embracing that shit and giving it back to her threefold, I need to step over her feelings and keep up appearances. Why? Because I need her emotions to be real when we face Paco. If that fucker knows what she really means to me, he'll see it as a challenge to finish what he started.

If I act like she's just a bitch on my arm, warming my bed while I fuck others against the wall, yeah… he would gloat in Ruby's face. In his point of view, that's how women should be treated.

Fuck me. I'm holding her magnificent breast in my hand that's a perfect fit. Her pussy is in my other, and my fingers are rewarded with her heat and wetness. Ruby's body is molded against mine. My front to her back. Made for me. I can't do this. I need her to know, but the risk I'm taking can screw this all up. And yet, the way she can fight, how she picked up the things Tarzan taught her…

My hands fall away and I step back.

She immediately spins around, and anger tightens her eyes. Her hands curl into fists at her sides, and I can tell she's ready to unleash some vile words in my direction.

Before that can happen, I lay it all out for her. Here goes nothing. "Wives warm the bed while the husband fucks every available pussy he likes. You're to be owned. I need for you to hate me, Ruby. You had that covered when I fucked up the first time. I need to keep that in place so I can't fucking tell you that I knew you were mine, and only mine, the first time I saw you. I can't tell you that my heart belongs to you. That my dick will never see the inside of another woman's pussy, ass or mouth. I can't tell you because you might react differently when we meet Paco. I can't afford that disadvantage."

Her hands unclench and she hitches them on her hips. "Then why the hell are you telling me this? Are you telling me this? God, you're confusing. You know what? Never mind. I had a mind fart. I'm back to hating your ass so we're fine, okay? All peachy.

I'm not a virgin anymore; you can fuck around all you want. I hate your muscled hard ass, but we're still going to kill Paco. Gotcha." She whirls around and grabs the gun. "Now teach me to shoot already."

Punch in the fucking gut. Yeah, I know I said I couldn't tell her that, but I did. Right? Fuck. She hates me now, so that's perfect, right? Stepping forward, my hands close around her wrists to slide her arms more firmly in front of her, aiming the gun.

My mouth lines up next to her ear. "Like I said, but clearly, you were listening but didn't hear me, you stole my heart the very instant I saw you. The whole marriage certificate is a statement thing? Yes that's true, but that's a tiny shadow on a solid golden ring that won't break. Now you better keep that Yegor's bitch from popping out from time to time. Not only so I can fuck you into the right state of mind, but also so we can wrap up Paco. Do my words penetrate now, Ruby?"

"Yes," She practically shudders against me. "Penetrate, check."

Oh, for fuck's sake.

"Focus." I growl and step away. "Squeeze, don't yank it."

She glances over her shoulder and raises a single well-groomed eyebrow.

Shit. "I'm talking about the trigger, not my dick, dammit. Eyes forward."

Ruby chuckles and returns her gaze in front of her. She fires a round and I can tell by the way her shoulders move, she actually enjoyed that. My suspicion is correct when she fires a few more rounds. When she places the gun back on the shelf, I can see she's set the safety in place. Good girl.

Pressing the button, I reel the target in and see she's not all that bad. Every bullet left a hole, which is good, especially for a beginner.

"Not bad for my first time, huh?" She practically glows as she bounces on her toes.

My dick is painfully hard at the inadvertent reminder. "Seems like every first time with you is glorious." I mutter while I clean up.

As soon as I finish, I guide her out of the room, through the hall and back up the stairs. I need to either fuck her hard or step away for a moment to create some distance. I'm on edge and with me, that's never a good thing.

"Now what?" Her voice is filled with frustration when she strolls into my room.

Yes, I've brought her all the way up here and I'm still standing in the doorway, still trying to make up my mind.

"I need to either go out for a while or fuck you raw." There. She asked, didn't she?

She crosses her arms in front of her chest. "If you intend to fuck someone else while you're out, don't bother coming back. I won't be here."

"I told you before, Ruby, my dick will never see the inside of another woman. You know what? That disrespect just ripped the decision right out of my hands. Strip and place the ass that belongs to me on the edge of the bed. Feet next to it and legs falling open. I want you on your fucking elbows enjoying

144

the view while I eat you out and ram my cock so far up your tight pussy, repeatedly, until I explode. For the rest of the day, every time you swallow you will taste my cum. That's how deep I'll brand you. *Fuck someone else.* You better not question my dick's loyalty; he and I don't condone that shit."

It's like my woman froze into an ice sculpture. Her eyes are wide, but without a hint of fear or annoyance. Nope, desire is plainly swirling in those dark depths.

"Now, Ruby. Clothes, bed." I bark and she jolts into action.

Stepping inside the room, I close the door and flip the lock. A few blinks of an eye and she's in position exactly how I told her.

"What a phenomenal view. Tell me, Ruby…did you shave that pussy for me? Because last time I saw it, I could have sworn there was a light patch of fluff on there. You wanted my mouth on you to experience every lick and suck to the fullest extent, did you now?"

The rapid rise and fall of her chest, the heavy scent of her arousal, and glistening folds are all a visual that shows me she likes the words I chose to vocally caress her.

"But you forgot one thing, Ruby. I liked that patch of fluff."

She sucks in a breath, her eyes widen.

"That's right. You stole something from me. That's my pussy, my body, my woman. You might brighten up your hair on your head to a fiery, screaming variation of the redhead you truly are and that's fine. From now on though, I'll be the one to handle the razor smoothing what's mine so I can bring back the dash of original fire between your legs."

I slide to my knees in front of my own piece of heaven. Placing a hand on each knee, I skim them toward her center until both thumbs stroke her entrance. I glide up and down her slick lips as I open her and lean in. My tongue licks from ass to clit, and I have to close my teeth around her nerve bomb to prevent her from lifting her tight ass off the mattress.

One of my arms curls around her leg, flattening my hand on her belly to keep her in place. With ease, I slip one finger inside her tight pussy while she clamps down and one of the sexiest sounds tumbles from her lips. My eyes are locked on hers as I watch them roll back and drift shut in pleasure.

Sucking her clit, I give a slight nip with my teeth and her walls clench in a beat that's music to my dick. I was hard a moment ago, but that doesn't compare to the state my dick's in now. My woman's cum is flowing into my mouth, my name spilling from her lips.

She's got a death grip on my head, as if I would ever voluntarily cease my actions right now. Fuck, I mean, if this very room was on fire, my mouth wouldn't leave this pussy. It's mine, and I won't stop until I have my fill. Whether it's with my mouth, fingers, or dick, I crave it.

"I demand you to keep coming, gorgeous. I love your taste and I'm thirsty for more. You need to orgasm at least two more times before I come so painfully hard inside you that I won't have a fucking breath in my lungs. You rile me up, unleash and trigger every cell in my body for the sole purpose of worshipping what belongs to me. That's it, you taste so damn sweet." My tongue slides deep inside her pussy, while I mentally curse myself for being mouthy while eating her out.

I intend to fully enjoy myself, and her. Teeth gliding back and forth over her clit. One digit out, two back in, curling slightly up. Ruby buckles within my tight grip while my chest fills with pride. How fucking lucky am I, to have a woman like Ruby?

I can't keep my dick behind the bars of my zipper any longer. Standing up, I reach for my belt and my slacks hit the ground after my shirt drops to the floor. With two arms beneath her knees, I slide her back to the middle of the bed.

I balance on one hand, take my dick in the other and I tap it against her clit. Ruby gasps and moans in between smacks. Her gaze is scorching my cock and the heat of it is threatening to draw my balls up and spray cum all over her. I can't have that. I want it deep inside her.

"Ruby. Eyes here, gorgeous." Her beautiful eyes, full of desire, turn to me at the sound of my words.

Sliding just the tip inside her tight, warm, and oh-so-wet pussy, I lean closer to her face. "I didn't use a condom last time, and I'm not going to start now. If you're on birth control, then you are going to stop right the fuck now."

It's non-negotiable. I never thought I would see the day when I'd want to knock up a chick. Even more, I didn't see the point in bringing children into this fucked-up world. With the childhood I've had? Hell no.

And yet there's a burning in my chest to see my woman's belly round with our child. Something we made. The two of us, connected for life, through life. So yes, I damn well want it ASAP.

Ruby bites her lip as she stares intently. "No birth control."

All I need.

"Fuuuuuuck." I groan in utter ecstasy as I bury myself deep inside her in one stroke.

Her hands reach for my ass and I feel her nails dig in, urging me forward. As if I fucking need the motivation. Slamming said ass back and forth to create the friction we both crave, I then freeze.

Ruby's eyes flash open as she gasps in confusion.

"That's right. Eyes on me, no matter how intense my dick is feeding your building orgasm. I own that pleasure, so you better give me your full attention until your body gives out and you have no other option but to crash into a sleep that's meant for you to recharge, and recharge only. Once you're rested, I'm going to repeat the action a few more times tonight."

She bites her lip and gives a slight nod, and I'm a goner. My hips start to thrust and pick up speed. When I pinch her left nipple, her walls flutter around my dick, so I make sure to repeat the action with the other hard nub.

"So close, Yegor, please." She meets my every slam forward, intensifying the slapping sounds of our bodies.

Sweat drips from my body and onto hers, where it mingles with the slick moisture that coats her skin. It's a prediction of what's to come. Our fluids entwining, to be mixed inside her body. Her head tilts back, and it's only then that her connection breaks with our eyes as her walls start to strangle my dick in rapid waves. I have no other option than to surrender to her enchanting spell and fill her up with hot strokes of cum.

It's final. She's rooted deep inside my heart, just as my cock is lodged inside her right now. The difference is, my dick will continue to be in and out, while my heart will never let her slip away. I might keep her inside this room for the next few days so my dick can spend as much time inside her too.

CHAPTER TEN

I'm alive so he can die.

Ruby

"Oh, come on, Ruby. It's going to be fine." Tarzan's voice filters through the bathroom door.

I'm not ready to come out yet. Glancing at my reflection in the floor-to-ceiling mirror, I barely manage to keep the nervous yelp inside my mouth. Yegor and I spent the last few days inside his bedroom. We didn't even leave for food. We just had it delivered to the door. We had ourselves a full blown sex-a-thon, only stopping for eating, sleeping and bathroom breaks. And yes, even bathroom breaks sometimes slipped into shower sex.

After spending the last few days naked, it feels strange to be wearing a dress. Specifically, an evening dress that's pitch black. Elegant silk strands flow from my waist down to my ankles. A split slices up my leg to the very top of my thigh.

The dress is so beautiful, I'm afraid to go downstairs. The sheer nude-toned high neck and long sleeves seem to disappear so all I see when I look in the mirror is the black flower detail wrapping around my arms, breasts and belly.

Not to mention, I'm wearing heels that look like jewelry. For real, they are beautiful. Like carved silver flowers molded into stilettos, with straps that wrap around my feet.

"Yegor is waiting for you downstairs. I'm right there with you. Hell...our whole gang is there. Open the door, Ruby." Tarzan keeps up her persistent knocking along with a firm voice.

I know I have to do this, so after one more deep breath, I flip the lock. Tarzan opens it immediately.

Strolling inside, her gaze connects with mine in the mirror, and her words tumble right out. "Wow, you look amazing."

Behind her, Karma, Peacock's wife, steps inside and her eyes widen. Even though I just met her, she has no problem telling me what she thinks. "Damn, you look hot."

"You girls," I groan. "This isn't helping. I mean, look at it. I'm afraid to take one freaking step. I bet this whole thing cost more that I made last year. And that's including tips during the summer when I worked as a waitress. Hell, I bet it's more than…"

"Okay, stop right there, missy." Tarzan points a finger at me. "You have to toss those thoughts in the garbage, because you're no longer in that life. Yegor is loaded, and therefore you're loaded. Man up, woman up, whatever you wanna call it, and get over yourself. Now, are there any other insecurities I need to destroy? Anything?" She raises her eyebrow in question and all I can do is smile.

"Nope. I think I'm good." I reply.

"Ah. Look at that. We kick ass in these dresses. And…we all know how to kick ass, in these dresses. Do you think our hubbies would mind if we ditch the party and head to the gym downstairs? I mean, there's a reason they have a split like this in a designer dress, right? Raising legs to head level is a necessity, you know." Karma smooths down her dress while she checks herself out in the mirror.

Karma is decked out a dark blue strapless A-line dress with peacock feathers embroidered across the torso. It fits her body perfectly. Tarzan is dressed in a bright cobalt blue halter dress with lace around her waist that shows some skin in peekaboo fashion. They both are wearing strappy sandals similar to mine.

"Killer heels, Karma. Remember, we just bought them, I don't want them ruined any time soon." Tarzan rolls her eyes and leans in. "Karma here likes to kill targets by jamming her heel into an artery. She's quite the hitman, you know."

"Retired, Tarzan…I'm retired. I only do that shit for pleasure now. But Peacock told me to behave, so that's why I said gym. Kick some rubber guy's ass, and it keeps everything squeaky clean." Karma's bright smile could light up the room.

I'm still nervous, but with these two girls having my back, I feel a little more settled. I know Yegor told me that most of the guests at tonight's party will be people from our own gang. Dammit…own gang. Months ago, I would have face palmed myself at the thought of becoming the wife of a mob guy and part of a mafia gang.

Yet all of it feels like I'm part of a family. I'm not alone anymore, and all of them look after one another. Ford and Tarzan both had their own gang and merged them into one huge gang. When you add Peacock's organization…yeah…lots of people. For an outsider, it might seem that it's a huge party. Yet every single one of them is on our side in this war. Well, except for Ricca and Paco. They were invited, along with a plus one and obviously, their right-hand man. But clearly, they are seriously outnumbered.

Centering myself with this knowledge…I realize I need to get over myself and get downstairs. Confront Paco on my own turf. Look him in the eye and shoot a fuck you through it. Show him I'm a warrior and he chose the wrong woman to fuck with.

"I'm ready." I announce firmly and full of determination.

"You are." Both girls agree.

We all stroll out the bathroom and head down the hall to the stairs.

"Let's do this, ladies. Remember to smile, Ruby. Always smile." Tarzan tells me.

Karma nods. "Yes, even when you stab a guy or hit his balls. A smile is crucial. We are after all ladies, right?"

I release a very unladylike snort.

"See," Karma says. Her smile is radiant. "Just like that."

The grin that's spreading across my face resembles theirs. "Thanks. You girls don't know how much this means to me."

"Aw, honey. We do. Believe me, we do." Tarzan strokes my back. "Now just slide your eyes over to the bottom left. That's your man right there, waiting for you."

Glancing over, I see Yegor standing with a firm grip on the banister. His knuckles are white and his face looks fierce and yet pained.

"He doesn't look all too happy to see me." I mumble, more to myself than to the girls standing beside me.

"Aw, honey…" Tarzan croons again. "Don't you see he can't believe his eyes? You're too gorgeous, too damn hot. I bet he wants to drag you off to that room he's kept you in for days and fuck you some more. Just as long as he doesn't need to share you walking around, looking all sexy, while other dudes gawk their eyes out."

"Damn." I mutter.

"Ah. Yes, damn. Look behind him. I believe he's not the only one with a look like that painted on his face." Karma chuckles.

Somehow that makes me feel good. I am damn lucky to have such support from all of them. We make our way down the stairs. Yegor takes my hand, as do each of the other men, grabbing hold of their own woman.

"Let's mingle." Ford mutters and we all follow him to the ballroom.

Huge doors are propped wide open and when we step inside, my breath catches when I catch sight of the beauty before me. Like the rest of the mansion, the room has been completely restored, right down to the amazing carved details in the twenty-foot ceiling.

It's straight out of a fairytale castle ballroom. Chrystal chandeliers, a marble dance floor...even the pillars that are scattered around the ballroom have carved details. People are sitting at the tables that are placed near the walls, leaving the center of the room open to dance or to just gather around in groups.

"Wow." I whisper.

Yegor squeezes my fingers softly. "That was the word that went through my head when I first laid eyes on you."

My gaze slants in his direction. "Just now, or the very first time you saw me?" I can't help but smile when I tease him.

"Both times, love," he tells me with complete honesty. "And those two times came with fury after that. Ready to pounce on anyone who dared to come near you or glanced at you."

This time I'm the one squeezing his fingers. "I'm yours, Yegor. Not one single person walking this earth holds a fraction of the love I feel for you. No worries about that, we're here to do a job and then… a few hours from now…we're going right back to our room. Right?"

"Another fuck marathon, you got it, Ruby. Damn. My dick is not liking my slacks right now. The teeth of my zipper is a killer for the hard-on I'm sporting. We need to stop talking about that shit for now. That and you need to dance with me to hide the boner." He grumbles, making me laugh and relax at the same time.

When the third song begins, Yegor guides me off the dance floor to a table in the left corner. Tarzan and Ford are sitting there, along with Afon and Borya. Next to Borya is Tori. She's wearing a stunning dark blue, or maybe close to purple evening dress with a plunging neckline. Her hair is tied up in a bun at the crook of her neck. There are pearls placed here and there in her dark hair. She looks amazing.

What's even more amazing? Borya is holding her hand that's placed on her thigh. Tori's body is slightly leaning toward his, and there's a smile on her face that's telling. It's clear that Borya stopped pushing Tori away and finally made his claim. Those two have been dancing around each other for weeks now. I think everybody knew they belonged together, but they just weren't ready. Until now.

"Finally. You took your time, Yegor." Ford's eyes slide from Yegor's to somewhere behind us. "They're both here. There's something going on between them, because they're sitting on opposite sides of the room. They haven't acknowledged each other, and yet they obviously know the other person is there. It's weird."

"No one thinks Ricca sounds girly? Because I sure as fuck think so." Afon grumbles before he takes a sip of water.

A snort drops in from behind us. Turning my head, I see Peacock standing within arm's reach. He's holding Karma possessively close to him, with an arm wrapped around her waist.

"I dare you to say that shit to his face. What would happen next would be very entertaining, I can tell you that." Peacock smooths a hand down his tie after he straightens the knot.

Afon's eyes slide to the corner, where Ricca is sitting with another man. "Maybe I will, but not until the party's almost over. That way he can keep his pretty face clean."

"Afon." Tarzan warns. "No one is going to kick anyone's ass." The corner of her mouth tips up. "Not unless I say so, anyways."

"Okay folks, get ready to have some mighty high times." Ford holds out his hand to Tarzan, who laces her fingers with his. "Here comes Paco."

My whole body freezes. Yegor's hand slides from my lower back to my hip and presses me close against him.

Leaning close, he whispers, "Remember, gorgeous. Just four bad guys and over a hundred of our guys in this room. Outnumbered is an understatement."

I appreciate the reminder that I'm not helpless. I can look Paco in the eye and shoot him down, and nothing would happen to me. Seriously. Well, maybe it would be a little hiccup if they needed to wipe out the guy who came with him. Or the floozy on his arm that he's dragging over to meet us.

I don't mean that as degrading or anything, but for real. All of the women attending this party are dressed to the nines. Full-length evening gowns, flawless hair and makeup. And gorgeous shoes. Classy. This one is wearing a fire-engine red, rhinestone halter dress that is so tight it's a wonder she's still breathing. Well, maybe it's because it's barely covering her pussy so the air flows in from the bottom, rather than the top. And judging by the size of her boobs, they might come equipped with oxygen tanks.

Ugh. I shake my head to rid the nasty thoughts. I'm a friendly person. I don't usually carry hate or judge people by their appearances. People might look shallow, but you should never judge the reasons for their actions. To each their own.

For now, I'm taking in the son of a bitch who threw hell at me. His thick black hair is combed back, slick and shiny. A light beard covers his tight jaw. He's wearing a dark blue suit and a white button down shirt that seems to be ripped open, showing off a lot of chest hair. Okay, that's so not sexy. I know many others can pull off that look, but on him? No way. He has something red tucked into his jacket pocket where a handkerchief goes. But seriously, maybe it's his chick's panties. Ew.

"Ford." Paco extends his hand for Ford to shake. "Thank you for the invitation. I foresee a solid connection for our gangs to work together. I appreciate you taking the first step. It's one I won't forget, and with that you have my respect and friendship."

I need to puke. And put a bullet in his head. I don't care in which order. Both are necessary, although I really hate puking.

"Ah, the choices we have to make that are a necessity for the path of the future." Ford says to Paco.

Ford doesn't accept the hand that Paco is still holding out, but instead waves at Yegor. "You've met my right hand, Yegor Volsky. *His wife*, Jude."

Paco spins around and it's as if he's seeing us for the first time tonight. His shoulders rear back and he seems to grow a few inches. Disgust and hatred fill his eyes when his gaze lands on Yegor.

"Ah, the son of a mere foot soldier, or so it's been said. You cleaned up nicely working underneath a boss, *mio fratello*."

My brother. Yuck. The way he says that word, he might as well add some vomit on the side.

The chick in the tight scrap of a dress wiggles around like she needs to pee.

When she speaks, her voice sounds like nails on a chalkboard. "Daddy, you promised we'd dance."

Daddy? For reals? *Daddy?* Oh, double yuck.

Paco taps the hand she set on his chest before his eyes slide to me. I can tell right away that he recognizes me. The feral smile on his face makes me swallow. I can't let fear overtake me. I'm safe here. I'm alive so he can die after I've kicked him down memory lane. And that's exactly where he's going. I might as well point him in the right direction.

CHAPTER ELEVEN

Don't push it, Russian.

YEGOR

I know she's about to blow when she goes from rigid to standing tall with pride. My fingers curl around that perfect waist and pull her tighter against me.

Lifting my chin, I point out, "Your piece of ass is asking for attention. Better go fill her up before she starts to leak on the marble floor."

The fucker narrows his eyes, and I can see the fire start to build inside him. My woman, on the other hand, is shaking against me. Not from fear, nope...she's struggling not to laugh. How do I know this? Because Karma and Tarzan are in my field of vision and have their eyes on Ruby, and they're both grinning like idiots.

Ruby's hand snakes up my chest to my jaw. When I look her way, her eyes lock with mine before her mouth inches closer. Her voice lowers to a whisper, yet she plainly intends for Paco to hear.

"It's a shame she'll never get a taste of what it's like to be fucked by a true man. Right, love? Because I definitely got the better brother." She nips my bottom lip and licks away the sting before she turns her attention to Paco and the chick standing next to him.

Instead of being offended, the chick seems to contemplate taking a step toward me. She turns to Paco with a pleading look on her face. What the fuck?

Paco nods. "Hmmm, I know what you're thinking and I like the suggestion. Let's see if my brother is willing to share more than some DNA, shall we?"

"Yeah, let's not before I let the DNA flow onto the marble floor." I growl.

A throat clears behind us. "Now, now, gentleman. Let's not spill blood before I get a chance to join in."

Turning around, and taking Ruby with me, I come face-to-face with Ricca. His eyes hold mine for an instant before they slide to my wife, and I see them widen when recognition sets in.

"Jude. What a delight to see you here." Ricca's voice does a one eighty; I bet he's going for husky.

I don't condone that shit regarding my wife. "Ricca. I believe you know my wife." Observing a woman in a light blue dress and a massive bundle of black curls coming up behind Ricca, I add, "Although we haven't met yours, but I believe that's about to change."

Ricca doesn't even glance behind him, his gaze locked on Ruby. "No, that's not my wife. That would be my sister, Andy."

"Dude's name sounds girly; girl's name sounds manly. Nice gender-swapping name thingie you folks got going there." Afon chuckles.

"Hell, yeah…here we go." Peacock's voice flows out in a sing-song voice.

We all focus on Ricca, but instead it's Andy who pushes him back and steps in front of her brother to come face-to-face with Afon. For a moment, she seems dumbstruck, but before Afon can take his next breath, his air supply is cut off by the fingers she's tightening around his neck.

"Is your Russian skull too thick to process the fact that *a girl* is standing before you, *carciofo*? Or are you confused by my manly grip?"

Did she call him *carciofo*? I'm pretty sure that means artichoke. But if I remember correctly, it can also be used as an insult. Clearly, Afon is all goo-goo eyes over the green-eyed beauty before him. Because he doesn't seems to need oxygen, or his brain is already deteriorating from lack of it.

"Your grip needs to slide a little lower if you want some manly strength, *anima mia*." Afon chuckles or maybe he's choking; I'm not getting a clear reading on the matter.

And for real…*anima mia*? My soul? He's throwing out Italian words. How the hell does he even knows what that means? Rather than having a positive effect on Andy, it seems to fuel her anger. Her hand releases his throat as she smacks her other palm against his cheek.

"*Vaffanculo!*" Andy seethes before she turns and walks off.

Afon's eyes follow her. "Fuck off? I'll show her,"

"I wouldn't do that if I were you." Ricca warns him.

Afon tilts his head to the left. "And why is that? You think you can take me?"

Tension charges the air. Borya's hand slides to the left side of his belt, as are mine and Ford's, in case we need to go for our guns.

All our actions halt when Ricca laughs. "It isn't me you have to worry about. It's her. Though she's my sister, I have to warn you. She wears double-edged knives on each of her thighs. I even think she's got little throwing stars hidden between safety patches in the straps of her bra. So go right ahead if that cut on your lip ain't enough blood for you."

Afon licks the cut on the left corner of his lip.

"Right, I forgot to mention she wears a large ring for the open-hand slap thing. It's something Andy kept from the time we were kids. She perfected it by practicing on me. So, from one dude to another, even though you mentioned my name might sound girly to you, I'll give you some slack..." Ricca doesn't have a chance to tell Afon more about his sister, because Paco rudely interrupts.

"Right, well...this is all very entertaining, but I'm bored and so is my little fuck hole. We'll be leaving." Paco turns his attention to Ford. "Thanks so much for your hospitality. It's been fun. I'll be sure to stay in touch."

Ford gives a curt nod before Paco strolls off, the bitch in heat trailing behind him while still throwing glances at my dick over her shoulder.

I feel Ruby step closer. "Eyes off, *puttana*," she mutters.

"Great, does everybody speak fucking Italian all of a sudden?" I grumble.

"Hey, you Russians aren't very friendly with all the judgement." Ricca sneers.

My hands come up in a display of defense. "Sorry, man. I'm just frustrated with that fucker who left."

"You and me both." Ricca's eyes slide to my woman.

"Okay, one more thing. She's mine, asshole. I'd appreciate it if you kept your eyes off her." My voice leaves no room for argument.

Now his hands come up. "Hey, I got ya the first time. It's just that when I asked her out the first time I saw her, she turned me down and told me politely that she didn't have time to date. Now, barely a few weeks, or hell, a few months later she's married? I'm just stunned, by her beauty, but also the fact that she's married."

Ruby steps up to Ricca and jabs a finger in his chest. "Yeah, well...I could say I owe it all to you."

Ricca's head rears back in shocked confusion. "Me? Why? How?"

"Because, you Italian mob idiot, you…it was you who put a bullseye on my head. You must have mentioned it somehow, or he found out. Fact is, Paco had me kidnapped by idiots who held me prisoner so he could fuck me before he slit my throat."

Ricca swallows hard as he clenches his fist, brings it up to his mouth, and bites down.

"No…" He mumbles against his fingers as he shakes his head in denial.

"What the hell is going on here?" Andy steps closer to her brother. "Ricca? What's wrong?"

Ricca's hand drops and his face slides into a sculptured resemblance of pure hatred. "Remember when we had the meeting with Paco a few weeks ago? The day I bought my new car and talked about the girl I met?"

"Yes." Andy answers, confusion written on her face. "You told us that she was the kind you would fall on your knees for, right?"

Ricca points a finger at my wife. "That's her. The one I told you about. They just told me that Paco had her kidnapped and threatened to rape and kill her."

"That asshole motherfucker," Andy snaps. "I knew I should have put a star in his eye when he put his paw on my tit."

"Left or right one?"

We all stare at Afon, who just popped out that question.

Andy squints her eyes. "Left or right, what?"

"Hand. What hand? So I know what fucking body part I'm gonna cut off first." Afon replies.

As in slow-motion, a smile so bright starts to spread on Andy's face. "See, that's how you get on my good side. You ain't half so bad, *carciofo*."

A satisfied grin slides across Afon's face. Fuck. I make a mental note not to tell him...

"You're aware she's still calling you a very naive person, right? Not totally stupid, but definitely one who's prone to be duped and conned. Because *carciofo* means artichoke, but it can easily be used as an insult." Ruby's eyebrows are raised as she informs

Afon.

He doesn't seem insulted at all. He just slides his tongue from left to right over his bottom lip. "Thanks for the translation, Ruby. I think I'll stick close to the source, though. We might learn something from one another."

Afon shoots a wink at Andy.

Her chin lowers as one eyebrow heads for the ceiling. "Yeah, don't push it, Russian. The moment is gone. As for that Paco fucker…He's going down."

"He sure as hell is." I growl.

"Couldn't agree more." Ricca adds. "At first, we had a meeting to start a line of shared transport across the border. One of my companies imports wines and olive oil, and he invited us over to talk about a business proposition. At the end of the meeting, he told us he would take over our connections. Clearly, he mistook me for a fool. It cost us eight of our guys against fifteen of his. If he…"

"I got this as a reminder," Andy slides away the right part of her top, barely keeping the nipple of her breast covered.

She reveals a deep, red, angry scar. It looks almost the same as the one on Afon's neck. A few weeks ago, the leader of the gang connected to the snuff movies sliced his throat. We almost lost him that day. Afon rubs two fingers against his neck, and Andy's eyes follow the movement. Her eyes widen a bit as she sees the reminder that he almost lost his life.

Afon steps closer to Andy, his hand crossing the distance between them as his finger hovers over her scar. "Mother-fucker. I'm going to dissect his dick and make sure to expose every nerve ending before I make him choke on his own blood."

"Aaaaand the moment is back." Andy whispers, while it's clear to me she's trying to keep her breathing steady. Failing, the scar on her breast rising and falling rapidly with each inhale and exhale.

"Back off, Afon. We're in the middle of business. Or you two can excuse yourselves so we can continue." Ford barks.

"Aw, you screwed up his moment," Tarzan says, sulking a little. "That's not nice. And I really like her too. She'll fit right in. Then we'll have four chicks. It evens the numbers, and we can work out in pairs. That's way better than if it's just the three of us."

Andy's head turns. "Oh, you must be Tarzan. I've heard about your mad rope skills. Pretty nifty. I'd love to workout with you guys."

"Yeah, you girls run along, so the guys can throw some weight around." Ricca grabs a chair and sits down.

Four sets of eyes skewer him in his seat.

"What?" He asks. He glances over at Ford. "What did I say?"

"Yeah, not helping you out, buddy. Every woman around here, well…maybe except for Tori here, because she's a nurse and even though she's a total badass, she has no mad fighting skills." Ford nods to Tori. "No disrespect intended."

Tori beams at Ford. "None taken."

Ford dips his chin in respect and proceeds. "All the others? Lethal. Even Ruby, Yegor's wife who you know as Jude…my woman taught her the ropes, so to speak."

Andy clears her throat and looks at Ricca. "I am so out of here. Brother, you take lead in this. Us women need to be excused. Fuck a bathroom break to patch up some makeup. We're gonna throw some knives and punches."

I feel Ruby's lips on my cheek and her hot breath in my ear. "Bye now, gotta go."

Before I can say something in return, the women hightail it out of the room.

"Fuck. Not that I want to be tied down anytime soon, but damn. That's kinda hot knowing a woman will drop a high-class party to go workout with other chicks." Ricca says, his gaze still fixed on the door the women just exited through.

"You and me both man." Afon adds and grabs a chair, drags it back, and takes a seat.

Time to get our heads together and work on a plan to bring Paco down.

CHAPTER TWELVE

A healthy flow of my cum.

Ruby

I'm soaking in the tub, letting the hot water relax my muscles. It's been an amazing night and that's something I never thought I'd say before the party started. We've even made a new friend. Andy is amazing. I've already learned a few things from her. Hell, even Tarzan picked up a thing or two.

Screw talking about shoes or lipstick…shit…we still do that, but it's more fun to talk about weapons or the best technique to bring a man down when he's behind you with his arms wrapped tight around you.

My phone buzzes, indicating I've got a message. We made a group chat so we can all stay in touch. For now, I leave my phone alone. I'll check the message when I get out of the tub in a few minutes.

My mind slips back to Yegor. He's not back from the party yet. The girls and I worked out for nearly two hours before we decided to call it a night. That's how I ended up in my room, wrapped in the delightful fragrance of vanilla and jasmine.

Okay, time to drag my sore ass out of this tub and into bed. Pulling the plug, the water begins to drain as I step out of the tub. Wrapping the world's softest towel around me, I glance over at my phone. After drying my finger, I tap a few times and catch up on the conversation.

Tarzan and Andy are planning to meet up in three days, though all four of us are invited. Karma replied that she was fine with any decision about time or day. They agreed to meet up tomorrow instead of waiting a few days. Tarzan seemed to take me not answering as the right to speak for me, deciding to meet at Yegor's house since he's got an amazing space to work out in.

Honestly, I don't mind. We sort of live in the same house. Besides, she's Yegor's boss…so therefore she's…my friend. Ha. Yeah, she's so not my boss, but it kicks ass to be friends with my husband's boss. It comes with all kinds of perks.

Like how I already know some of the information that was discussed by the men while we were working out. Tarzan thinks I need to know everything. She asked me how much I thought I could handle first, but, hello…she taught me to fight, building my confidence and abilities, so I sure as hell am ready for everything. I need to know, because not knowing and imagining the worst…yeah, not helping. That earned me the brightest of smiles.

Tossing the towel in the hamper, I stroll out of the room and see it's still empty. No sign of Yegor. My shoulders slump. It's weird how I can go from sleeping alone all my life to waking up next to my husband the last few days.

Strolling over to his closet, I take out one of his t-shirts and put it on. The moment my head hits the pillow, sleep catches me.

The fresh scent of lime, sandalwood, cinnamon, and a subtle aroma of red berries fill my nose. Yegor. It's something my nose and body recognize as safe, home, my man. Then there's the feel of his strong arms wrapping around me and his muscled body curling around mine.

I don't want to open my eyes. My voice is groggy when I ask. "What time is it?"

Yegor buries his face in my neck, softly feathering kisses. "Go back to sleep, gorgeous. I'm beat. We have a few more hours of sleep before we get up, 'kay?"

"Hmmhmmm." I manage as an answer before my whole body relaxes with the comfort only he gives me.

I could swear someone is massaging my right ass

cheek. Then again, I might be dreaming. The moan that slips from my mouth enters my ear. Yeah, not so much sleeping, am I?

"Fuck, you feel so good." Yegor whispers while his hand slides lower and grazes my clit.

"Oh, yes. Now that feels good." I hum and push my ass back, but then freeze when I feel the tip of his dick against my asshole.

Now it's his turn to hum. "Couldn't agree more."

"I can't." Shit.

My whole body locks down. He's not seriously thinking about shoving his dick up there, is he?

"Relax, Ruby. It's not like I can jam my dick up there without any preparation first." Yegor croons.

Preparation. Jam his...

"Yeah, that's a no-go zone, asshole." I state.

Now he actually chuckles. "Ruby..." His fingers dance over my skin, and I swear electricity is bouncing off, igniting goosebumps all over my body. "Let me show you that I only intend to bring you pleasure."

His body disappears from behind me as he pushes me gently down on my back. His mouth covers my nipple. His sucking and nipping makes it hard to keep my body from thrashing around.

My hands grasp his hair to keep him in place, while my legs close around his thigh. Shamelessly I ride it, creating a delicious friction for my clit. His growl rumbles though his chest, the sound so sexy that the next bite on my nipple sends a sharp jolt between my legs. My whole body tightens and explodes into an orgasm that makes me shudder.

Yegor lifts his head and blows out his breath, making my nipple tingle from the combination of air and wetness. "Used me to get yourself off, did you now."

Not a question. A statement. And if he's throwing that out to see if it shames me, then he's going to be disappointed.

"Damn right. Now, do it again, husband." I demand before I try to guide his head to my other nipple that's been getting no attention at all and feels a little left out.

His hand lifts and he freaking twists my nipple. Yes, the one that was feeling left out. Guess it's quite the opposite right now.

"You don't get to order me around in bed, Ruby. Watch your mouth or I'll fill it up and silence you with a healthy flow of my cum." His eyes slide down to my mouth. "Don't fucking lick your lips, dammit." He growls at me. "I'm going to eat that sweet pussy first. Then I'm going to fuck you hard while you're on your hands and knees. I'm going to put my thumb up your ass so we can start preparing that tight ring for when my cock finally finds your back door."

He actually laughs at my sharp intake of breath. "That's right, gorgeous. You're going to feel how it's like to be mine in every way. But first..."

He slowly makes his way down my body, putting his teeth on my skin every now and then, and my breath quickens with every nip. Yegor's eyes burn into mine as I watch his tongue sliding through my pussy. The tip flips back and forth over my clit before he covers it with his whole mouth and starts to suck.

"Oh, damn, I'm going to…" I'm almost there and the idiot rips his mouth away. "Aaahh! What the hell are you doing? Put it back!"

His head dips and I'm smiling internally, but only for a split second before he nips my freaking clit, making me yelp. "What the hell?"

"You're not allowed to come. Did you hear me say you could? No. You already got yourself off, so now it's up to me to give you what you need. And I'm telling you, you're not ready." He tells me this with a freaking straight face.

As if my whole body wasn't on edge, ready to tip over into a freaking bowl of happiness, glitter, and clouds of tingles. Not. Ready. I was born ready, dammit.

I flop down on my back instead of being propped up on my elbows, enjoying the view. Because the satisfied grin on his face is not one I'd like to see. Even though it's hiding against my pussy, I can still see it in his eyes.

Slinging my arms sideways, I take a deep breath. "All yours, pretty boy. Do your worst." There's a hint of annoyance in my voice I fail to hide, because really, he just did with taking away my chance to orgasm.

A powerful surge of heat spreads from between my legs all the way up through my body when his mouth covers my pussy and his tongue begins to flutter around my clit. I can feel his thumbs spread me open and his finger starts to pump inside. One of his hands snake underneath my leg, up my side and pinches my nipple.

The sweet combination of pain and pleasure almost sends me over. But there are teeth holding my clit hostage as I hear Yegor growl, reminding me I have to wait for his order.

Resisting the orgasm is getting harder and harder with every lick, pinch, and the way he pumps his fingers deep inside me. I've cursed him out like twelve times in a row already. Curling his fingers, he finds my sweet spot.

"Please, Yegor...I can't...please." I switched to begging when the first nine times of swearing only made him work harder and then back off when I almost tipped over. A few more swears and now I'm begging some more.

Suddenly, Yegor raises his body and hoovers over my face. "All right, gorgeous." He croons while his fingers are sliding in and out of my pussy, rotating between pumping and circling my clit.

His eyes are burning straight into mine. His chin is glistening with my wetness, his...aw fuck.

"Now, Ruby. Come for me." His permission flows through the air, and I surrender to the loud bells that are clearly ringing in the whole capital.

It's like I'm wrapped in white heat, while my body can only surrender to the pleasure. I didn't think it was possible to come that hard. Even though it was a very frustrating road to get there...being tortured with pleasure is after all still torture...I have to say he was right. The buildup led to an orgasm explosion of epic proportion. Like hell I'm going to tell him he was right, though.

My mental rant comes to an abrupt halt when Yegor flips me over. He grabs my hips and throws my ass in the air. My knees dig into the mattress as I hold my upper body up on my elbows.

Glancing over my shoulder, I see the magnificent man that's my husband. He's holding his dick in a tight grip while he's slowly pumping up and down. His other hand is rubbing circles on my ass, spreading heat all over my skin.

He's not even touching my pussy and yet, with the reminder of that mind-blowing orgasm, and the way he's standing there, eyes fixed on the place between my legs? That place throbs like hell, making me feel empty, longing for him.

"Please…" I whimper.

The hand that was caressing my ass leaves my skin for a heartbeat before it lands right back with a sharp sting.

"Aw, look at that. Fuck…your ass is mine, Ruby. My handprint scorches your skin in a delicate red. So fucking gorgeous. Slick pussy, clenching in anticipation. All ready for my cock to slide right in and light it up enough to rip my cum right out. But first,"

His thumb slides through my folds, dragging wetness along, skimming up to rim my asshole. "This tight little ring will be mine too."

I gasp when he starts to push in, moving forward in an effort to get away from him.

Yegor places his other hand on my hip, keeping me in place. His dick is hot against me while I feel the heat of his body as he hovers over me.

"Did you really think that tiny orgasm was the best one yet, Ruby? If that's the case, you're terribly mistaken. You'll love my thumb up your ass. My dick up that tight pussy will feel even tighter, because I'll be pumping that ass of yours, feeling my cock slide in and out of your cunt between a thin layer. Once I've fucked you like that, you'll beg me to fuck your ass next time. I'll even buy some toys for us to play with. Get one of those g-spot vibrators to slide into my pussy, so she's taken good care of while I'm fucking your tight hole."

Somewhere along his murmured words, I began to relax and even pushed back, impaling myself over and over on his thumb. The burning sensation I felt at first is long forgotten and replaced by a need. Some of it fades when the head of his dick nudges my entrance.

Thrusting forward, he buries himself deep in one stroke, filling both my ass and my pussy. I can only surrender to what I have to classify as the mother of the orgasm that went through my body before this one. Holy hell, how can it be?

Yegor starts to rock his hips and at the same time finds a rhythm for his thumb to work in opposite movements. The moans that leave my lips are answered by his deep grunts. I'm so wet from my orgasms that the sound of skin slapping is bouncing off the walls.

Yegor's hand on my hip slides up my spine to my shoulder, where he grips hard, keeping me in place so he can fuck me harder. His thumb is lodged deep in my ass, no longer pumping in and out, he looks like he's lost focus and solely chases his orgasm.

I manage to turn my head slightly to get a glimpse of how he's fucking me. His hand tightens on my shoulder. His dick grows harder inside me before I feel it start to pulse. Yegor grunts low from within his chest before my name rips from his lips. His eyes close and his head tips back while his hips are thrusted forward.

Another orgasm slams through me, and somewhere in the back of my mind it registers that Yegor is cursing because of the way my walls are clamping down on his dick. Completely spent, I slump down on the mattress in utter exhaustion.

CHAPTER THIRTEEN

A pretty bunch of cunts.

YEGOR

After lingering in bed for another two hours, we shower and dress. I couldn't resist sliding back inside her, so I took her against the tiled shower wall. I don't think I'll ever get enough of her. For now though, we need to get some shit done. I've already filled her in on what was decided late last night.

It seems that information is still processing in her head when she grabs her jacket and asks, "So, it's really happening?"

I can't help but fucking smile. "Yes, Ruby. I'm going to walk right into his office and put a bullet right between his eyes."

"Wow." She breathes in admiration.

I'm so damn proud to call her my wife. I'm also proud to be a part of the Dudnik Circle. My bosses don't just back me up, no…they make shit happen the way I like it to be played out. It's not normally like that, but in this case…Ford went out of his way to get this done.

This is not only business, it's personal. For me anyway, and also for my bosses. I know Ruby was with the girls and only one boss was present, but I knew Tarzan wasn't going to keep the information from her.

It didn't really matter, because I already made up my mind to keep Ruby informed about every little detail. She's proven herself plenty of times that she can keep it together and most of all, she can handle herself when shit hits the fan.

Doesn't mean I didn't catch the hint of disappointment in her eyes when I told her I needed to do it alone. It was there before she blinked it away, giving me a curt nod in agreement, adding that she understood because it was my half-brother. Then she went and tossed in that it was also my job as a husband to handle those things. Fuck. Like I said, damn proud.

"Seven more days. He gets to enjoy just seven more days on earth before his time is up." Ruby says.

Diminishing the distance between us, I take her face in my hands. "Seven days. We need time to set things up. I can't just walk in there, kill the fucker and walk back out. The path has to be cleared first so I can return safely back to you."

"That's more important." She whispers, while her gaze is locked on my mouth. "I can't imagine my life without you anymore, so you better get back to me safe and sound."

"I intend to, Ruby. I love you too much to stop breathing."

"Wow." She breathes again, but this time with a whole different kind of admiration.

Leaning in, I'm a hair away from devouring her mouth before she flips the intense words back at me. "I love you so freaking much, Studly."

Her hands roam my chest and dig into the fabric of my shirt to draw me closer while my tongue fucks her mouth.

With great reluctance, I pull back. "That's it for now, Ruby. Either that or I'll bend you over the bed and fuck your ass right now."

I can tell by the look in her eyes that she's about to step toward the damn bed. "Not happening, Ruby. You already arranged for the girls to meet at our place to work out, so I can dive into the file that's in my office, along with the blueprints of the house that our computer team sent over."

"Shit." Ruby stomps her foot. "Almost forgot. Well, Tarzan has a key, and I bet she's already at the house setting things up. Karma and Andy will be there in about," She checks her watch. "Twenty minutes or so. So, that leaves…"

"No." I growl and cross the room to grab my bag.

"We're leaving now, because I'm not ready to start having quickies with you. That shit will be saved for the second we have kids and actually need to speed things up. Until then I'll take my time worshipping that pussy, mouth, ass, and tits."

"Alrighty then. Well...I can work with frustration, you know. I can just take it all out on Tarzan, hit her hard and..."

"Gorgeous?" I wait for her gaze to connect with mine. "Don't share what you'll be doing with my boss, because both of my heads can't deal with it. The top one can't process the fact that you guys are kicking each other's ass, and the head between my legs can only process the part where the two of you get it on. Hot and sweaty, grunting, yeah...believe me, not something I want to deal with."

Her lips purse before she nods in understanding. "Got it." She beams a smile right at me. "Hot and sweaty with your boss."

She's fucking lucky she has good reflexes, because I was going to smack that tight little ass of hers.

"No, no...we don't have time for it, remember? We need to get home and....hot and sweaty." She throws over her shoulder while she leaves the room.

Fucking tease.

When we finally drive through the gate of our mansion, I don't see any of the girls' cars. "You sure about them coming over?"

I glance to my right to see Ruby has her thumbs dancing across her iPhone. "Yeah, I told them to park out back. Tarzan's been doing that ever since I moved in here."

"Why?" I ask, confused, because I always park in front of my house, or use the tiny garage on the right. I had that built two years ago because I needed more space, and yes...I'm lazy.

Her gaze flicks away from her phone. "Because, silly you have a monstrous garage back there. Plus, it connects with the gym across a tiny hallway. It's just easier that way. Why do you ask? Are you worried she's gonna scratch your cars or something?"

It seems we both have a thing for keeping it

simple and easy. "Nah, I never use that garage unless I'm unleashing one of my beasts."

"Hmmm." Ruby hums. "When you say it like that, the first thing that pops in my mind is your dick, or your tongue, or maybe even your fingers...but not one of your flashy sport cars."

"I created a horny monster." I mutter, absolutely content by the way she has no shame in voicing her desires.

We both slide out of the car, and I grab my bag that was in the front next to Ruby's feet and lock the car. We make our way toward the door. Hell yes, I parked out front. Didn't even put it in the garage. I mentioned I'm lazy, right?

I slide my bag off my shoulder, grab the blueprints that are stashed in a tube, and throw the bag near the stairs.

"You know where to find me." I tell her and plant a kiss on those lovely lips that belong to me.

Ruby grabs my shirt, preventing me from slipping away, so she can steal another kiss. "Right back at ya. I'm gonna go kick some ass."

"Have fun with the girls, gorgeous." I take a step in the direction of my office before I add over my shoulder, "Oh, and Ford told me he'd come by later with Afon and Peacock."

Ruby's eyes are fixed on her iPhone screen. "I know, Tarzan just told me." She holds up her phone. "Andy said Ricca will be here later too."

Nodding, I cross the foyer and head for my office. I need some time to review the blueprints of Paco's house. There's enough time to go through it before the day comes when I get to walk in and kill the fucker, but I like to be prepared.

I like to know the inside and outside of a house, building, boat, whatever it might be, before I go in. That way in case something happens, I know every exit there is and not get lost in the process. We discussed the seven-day timeline last night. That leaves enough time to plan correctly. At this moment, there are four people placed strategically around Paco's house. We need to know his routine, and how many men he has stationed inside and outside the house.

We also need to know how many people work for him, what his staff's like, when they pick up the garbage, and when the mailman drops by. That kind of shit. It's easy to walk in, kill everyone on sight, and stroll right out. But it does get a little messy. This way, we'll know the perfect time and maybe find an open window of opportunity.

After examining the blueprints for over an hour, I can literally close my eyes and mentally walk through the house. If everything goes right, I can be in and out of his mansion in less than three minutes. It only takes a steady breath to pull the trigger, so make it five and I'm in my car heading home.

Peacock suggested we use three of his men. He's got the best hitman on his payroll, so we'd be a fool not to use them. Ricca offered to have twelve of his men in three cars nearby and another fifty on standby. Add in our gang, which is double the size of their organizations, and you might say we're well prepared.

Okay, one more time. I lift my hand up to rub my

neck, and damn…I've been bent over this desk for too long. Maybe I need to check up on my wife and her friends, get a little workout in to stretch out some of those muscles, because…

"Well, well, well…not much of a security system there, brother. I bypassed that one without even making an effort. You should get yourself a dog." Paco's voice has my head jerking up. My gun is half raised when he clicks his tongue.

"No, no, put it down. I don't want to take you out right now. That would take away the fun I've got planned. Marco, would you be so kind to hold my brother at gunpoint so I can tell him a little story?"

Three men step up from behind Paco. One guy, who must be Marco, points his gun right at me. Paco glances over his guys and tucks away his gun.

Smoothing his hands over his gray suit, he takes a seat on the opposite side of my desk. "Right. I figured we could use a little bonding time."

My head is jumping from one thought to the other. Calculating every risk, every possibility to nail him and his guys. I hope to fuck he doesn't know the girls are here. Or maybe the girls spotted Paco and plan to take action or some shit.

"But first…" Paco's head turns toward the door.

Fuck. In strolls Tarzan, Karma, Ruby, and Andy. And they look pissed as hell, all four with their arms crossed in front of their chests. Three more guys follow after them, each with their guns drawn.

"There they are. Ain't you a pretty bunch of cunts?" Paco sneers.

Tarzan raises her hand, examines her nails, and rubs them on her sports bra as if she's polishing them out of utter boredom. I'm surprised they are all walking in here without a fuss, because my boss, Tarzan, can take three guys at once. And yes, with weapons drawn.

She's been training Ruby so she can handle herself and then add Karma, who's a hitman. Andy? I don't know her well, but from what her brother mentioned last night, I'm sure she can hold her ground. It doesn't make a lick of sense.

"Ah, that reminds me. The little fuck hole I was with last night? You might want to drag her body out of the pond next to Ford's house. I snapped her neck on the way out. She was annoying the hell out of me. Besides, I had business to handle." Paco leans forward and rips away the blueprint on my desk. "Ah, seems we were doing the same things. Only you're a little slow, brother. It might be because you're getting old."

Karma's phone starts to ring.

"Turn it off." Paco snaps.

Karma shakes her head. "No can do. I'm pregnant and my husband told me to meet him for lunch. He's expecting me in twenty minutes. He always calls so he can order for me ahead of time. Now, I can either answer the call to tell him I'm running late, or ignore it and get him angry enough to come and get me. He loves to spank my ass to remind me that I need to pick up my phone when he calls."

Paco starts to bark out his words. "I want two guns aimed at her head. Answer the phone, puttana. But one wrong word…"

"Yeah, yeah," Karma waves her hand dismissively and answers her phone. "Hey little dove….No, I can't make it. I'll be…six..ty minutes…yes that's one, dove, one hour. Yes, I'm hungry. You know how I love to…eat. Bye, bye." Karma holds up her phone. "There, happy now?"

Good fucking girl. Six and one. Seven fucking intruders. And for her to call her man dove? I bet he's going to spank her ass for calling her man a flying rat while his nickname is Peacock.

For an outsider, it might seem I'm alone in this fucked-up circumstances. Yet I'm standing here with my boss and three other trained individuals. It's still five against seven, with weapons pointed at us, but for real…to me that's not an end of the world situation. It's one that has possibilities. Besides, I never give up. Not until death prevents me from doing so.

CHAPTER FOURTEEN

The will to die.

Ruby

I wish I had a gun in my hand. And there are so many in this room, but none of them are within my reach. Well, maybe the one that's pointed at me, but Tarzan gave me the slightest shake of her head, telling me it was a no-go.

It is so very frustrating to be standing here and do nothing. Nothing! While the idiot who's to blame for all of it is sitting a few feet from me, babbling away to my husband as if he's taking a trip down memory lane.

The only positive point is that backup is on the way. The call Karma just took? Perfect. Letting her husband know something is up and even managed to tell him how many men were here. But the scary thing is she didn't lie…she really is pregnant.

"Which one of them?" a rough voice asks as a slick-haired man steps toward us. His eyes travel over us and land on Andy. "How about the one with the nice rack and curls?"

Paco nods while he keeps staring at Yegor, but his words are meant for Marco. "That's good, brother. See, Yegor? Marco and I share the correct set of DNA. Not the tainted one you and I share with our whore of a mother. I think it's time you heard the truth. You've been lied to all along. But first…Marco, take the woman. We need a hostage in a different location in case someone thinks they can storm in and ruin things."

Marco takes a zip tie from his pocket and grabs Andy's wrists, locks them behind her back, and snaps them together. Marco pushes her out the door, disappearing from view.

"My little brother, Marco, was born a month after me. We've always been together, raised by our uncle. His mother died in childbirth. It happens sometimes. Not like our mother, who killed herself after she had me. What was the story that they told you when you turned sixteen? When your uncle told you it was time for you to hear the truth. Right... that our mother couldn't go on living like that. After all, when she had you, they made sure that her belly was strapped tight and that there was no trace of her ever being pregnant." Paco clicks his tongue in disapproval.

Yegor's hands ball into fists on top of his desk. Judging by the way anger rolls off him, Paco is telling the truth. It takes everything in me to keep rooted.

Paco continues. "As the only daughter of a large gang leader, our mother needed to wed an appropriate man, one that fits her standards and could benefit the family. Your father, a mere foot soldier was killed the night they found out about the pregnancy, did you know that? Then they sent that whore you call a mother to marry my father, a Dom. Her own family was aware that my father would be furious on the wedding night. I mean, what decent Italian man wouldn't be when he found out he'd been lied to? Expecting a virgin, but getting a whore who's already spread her legs. Served him fucking right to rape her. He had to keep her locked inside his house, tied to a bed until she gave birth to me. The story goes that she ran off. That she killed herself. But the truth is my father had her dumped on the doorstep of her parents' house like the trash she was. He only needed me, an Italian blue-blood."

"Bringing up the past doesn't change the future." Yegor bites out his words as if it's the last thing he will every say about it.

Paco's smile turns feral. "Doesn't change the future? Just wait a moment, brother. The truth is a bit different than the one you've been told. They didn't want you to rip open something that was settled by elders. My father was murdered because of what he did, and with that, it was settled. Your real father wasn't a foot soldier, Yegor. He was a Dom; you're an Italian blue-blood too. How does that sound? To know that your mother was kidnapped and raped by my father? Kept hostage until I was born. Then they dropped her off in front of your real father's house. She was broken. Your daddy was devastated but intensely happy to have her back. But she hated herself, couldn't handle giving birth to the enemy's son. My father didn't want the puttana near me, another thing that was ripped away from her. So yes, she killed herself. But there's a difference in killing yourself even if the results lead to the same lifeless thing. They found her hanging on a low branch. She had to pull up her own feet to hang herself. That takes courage and strength, the will to die. They even found cuts on her throat from a knife that was near the body...she wanted, no, needed to die, with complete surrender and devotion. *She pulled up her own fucking legs to cut off her air supply.*

It's only in death that I respect the last and final thing our mother did."

Paco stands up and smooths his suit jacket and closes the button. "Now tell me, brother...does the past matter?"

"No." Yegor's voice lacks any emotion. It's cold, oh so cold. "The future is already set to have no place for you in it."

Paco throws his head back and laughs. "I believe you're mistaken. You're the one with all the guns pointed at you. Within the next few minutes, your life will end, and I will finally be rid of the last piece of rotten DNA that was mixed with mine."

"Wouldn't be so sure about that." Karma mutters beside me.

Paco's head snaps in her direction. "What was that, little fuck hole?"

"Christ. You really could use a vent to that tiny brain of yours. A little fresh air would be prefect to blow away the asshole inside you. Oh, look, right on the dot." Karma points at him.

All eyes in the room slide to Paco when we hear glass shatter and see his body jerk to the left before he lunges to the ground. The distraction enables Tarzan to take out the guy next to her. She grabs his wrist that's holding the gun with her left hand and punches him straight in the chest, followed by one underneath his chin. The gun falls to the ground. She switches to throw a blow against his jaw, then grabs his wrist again and kicks him to the floor. One down.

Karma snaps another man's neck just as the three other thugs lunge at us. Apparently, they choose hand-to-hand combat because they can't risk putting a bullet in one of their own guys. And that gives us the advantage we need.

From the corner of my eye, I see Yegor and Paco fighting. Actually, it looks more like Yegor is the one throwing punches. One man makes a move to kick Karma in the stomach, and acting on instinct, I step forward and kick him straight in the knee, causing him to fall down. That grants me the opportunity to jab my elbow in this neck and knee him in the face.

The sound of gunshots bounce off the walls, making my gaze dart around the room, searching for the source of the threat. I see Peacock standing in the doorway along with Ford. Afon and Ricca come running past them. The hatred in his eyes and the gun in his hand indicate it was Peacock who shot the remaining guys.

Grunts are still coming from the scuffling brothers. Yegor is punching the shit out of Paco. At least… what's left of Paco, because I'm sure they will have a hard time identifying him. No one can tell if that blob on his shoulders is supposed to be a face. Hell, I bet all his teeth are missing, which would make identification difficult.

Stepping forward, I move to stop Yegor, because this can't go on like this. I'm held back by Ford and Afon.

"Wouldn't do that if I were you." Ford tells me. "He's not with us right now. Let him ride it out."

I hear what they're saying but, really? Are they seeing what I'm seeing? Dammit, if this guy's face is pulp, I don't even want to think about what Yegor's fist looks or feels like.

"Where's Andy?" Ricca asks.

"Shit. Paco's brother, Marco, took her. They needed her as a hostage, insurance or some shit." Tarzan informs them.

Ricca takes out his phone and taps away while he turns, racing for the door.

"She's got a chip in her arm. I'll...shit. She's on the move." Ricca throws over his shoulder. Afon runs after him. Peacock, who was kneeling next to Karma, stands up.

"No," Ford holds up his hand. "You stay here, I got this. Tarzan. Eyes open." Ford rumbles as he joins Ricca and Afon.

Yegor is still beating one fist after the other into Paco. Grunting hard with each blow. Although the force of them have diminished a bit.

Soft mumbling makes my gaze switch to Karma and Peacock. He's stroking her back. Karma doesn't look too good. Shit.

I kneel down next to her. "Are you okay? Do you need to go to the hospital?"

Peacock gives me a tight smile. "Thanks for your concern, but she's positive nothing touched her stomach. Well, not coming from the outside anyway. Karma suffers from morning sickness. It comes and goes, and with all this stress and kicking some ass, she needs to sit and let it pass."

"Oh, thank fuck." I breathe. For a moment there I thought she might have been...

Karma grabs my forearm. "No, thank you. I saw how you blocked that guy. I'm sure he would have struck me in the stomach."

My hand covers hers as I give her a thankful squeeze.

"Uhmmmm, Ruby? You might want to do something right about now." Tarzan whispers next to me.

Turning, I see Yegor has stopped throwing punches. His ass is resting on his heels, while his upper body heaves with each labored breath.

"Yegor?" I walk slowly toward him.

He doesn't respond to my voice, so I call out to him once more. Again, nothing.

Reaching out, I lay a hand on his shoulder. The next instant, he surges up and his hand is wrapped around my waist, bringing me down. I see his other arm going back, ready to strike. My hand goes to his throat, cutting off his air supply while I bellow his name. "Yegor!"

His head rears back as if he's been slapped out of it. His eyes are no longer black darkness. His shoulders sag as he drags my body against him. My arm, stuck between our bodies, releases his neck. Yegor starts to shake as we both fall to the ground, clinging to each other.

I have no clue how long we sit like this, but when I hear a murmur of voices, I lean back and see Karma, Peacock, and Tarzan huddled in a circle, talking to three new men. Tarzan is clearly giving directions as they start to walk toward a body on the floor and start to clean up. As I take in my surroundings, I notice that I'm sitting on Paco's hand. Oh, gross.

Taking Yegor's face between my hands, I make sure his eyes are locked with mine. "Come on, Studly. We need a shower. Big boys are coming in for a cleanup. Let's make this easier for them, okay?"

His lips twitch and his nose rubs against mine. "I could use a hot shower. And you."

My head swings back to Tarzan and the rest of the guys.

"Everybody relax; he's back to his horny self again." I yell.

All eyes land on us. Peacock snorts as Karma chuckles. Tarzan just shakes her head.

Yegor's breath is hot near my ear. "You're gonna pay for that."

Acting shocked, I gasp. "What did I do? You're the one who went all Hulk mode. Flipped the switch back to fucking just now. I might make you flip the switch while we're fucking so you can pound..."

I can't finish that sentence because he twists my nipple, making me curl my lips around my teeth and bite down, preventing me from screaming out.

"No worries, gorgeous. I'll have you screaming out in no time." Yegor says.

Tarzan's phone rings, preventing me from a snarky comeback. She answers the call, but I can't make out what the discussion is all about.

"I hope they found Andy." I mutter the first thing that still has my worry.

"Shit." Yegor curses some more and stumbles closer to Tarzan, bringing me with him.

We both wait patiently until Tarzan finishes the call and turns to us. There's sadness on her face.

"They found her. Andy managed to escape."

"Thank fuck." Yegor mumbles.

"Yeah, not exactly. She jumped out of a moving van. Her hands were still tied behind her back. She's at the hospital, but they don't have any update other than it doesn't look good." Tarzan swallows.

I cover my face with my hands. Shit. How could she do that? Jump out of a speeding van? Yegor wraps his strong arms around me, rocking me back and forth.

"Let's clean up, let the guys clear this room in the meantime so we can head over to the hospital, huh?" Yegor kisses my neck.

My hands slide down, and I lace my fingers with his as he guides me out of the room and up the stairs.

CHAPTER FIFTEEN

We make our own choices.

YEGOR

"Are you okay?" Ruby's voice rips me out of my thoughts.

We're all waiting in one of those clinical waiting rooms with just a few chairs, a table with magazines, and some paintings on the wall. I've been going over things in my mind ever since I planted my ass on this seat.

That was after they told us Andy was in surgery. She has a shoulder injury, serious bruises, and severe road rash. They were concerned about a head injury, but it sounds like her shoulder is the worst of it. Well, not so lucky to have a splintered shoulder they need hours and fucking hours of operating to see if they can reconstruct it.

But am I fine? "Yeah. Don't worry about me."

Ruby's delicate hand slides back and forth over my thigh. "Sure, Studly. Sure, you're fine."

Normally, she would lace her fingers with mine, but I'm wearing gloves and my hands throb like crazy. It's a delicious reminder of my release of built up fury and frustration. Thankfully, I was able to kill my half-brother. But deep down it's not enough. I want to kill him over and over again. And then some fucking more.

Getting to my feet, I stare down at Ruby. "I'm not fine. But I will be once I kill that fucking guy who ran off. That would be a nice start."

"Sit your fucking ass down. No one is touching that dick but me." Afon growls. "If I have to sit my ass on this hard as a rock seat, then so will you."

"Nobody is killing anyone." Peacock's voice is steady. "Remember where we are people; they save lives here. Besides…I already put in a call to the Italian syndicate. As a spokesperson for the top Russian gangs within the US, it's my duty to report an incident. Fuck incident. A flat out hit on one of our own guys, risking my pregnant wife, two other high ranking women, and putting another one in the hospital. This fuck-stick better be hiding in a hole somewhere, because his ass is now the biggest target on the fucking planet."

"The fucker needs to keep breathing so I can find him and rip his lungs out. Fuck the syndicate, he's mine." Afon snaps.

"Cool it, Afon." Tarzan tries to reign him in, but it's apparent that no one will be able to diminish that fire.

Earlier, we had to drag him out of the emergency room as they wheeled her out for surgery. He didn't want to leave Andy, even when they assured him that she would pull through.

Ricca has gone out of his way to make sure Afon is in the thick of things. He told the doctors Afon was his sister's fiancé, making sure Afon is allowed to see her once she's out of surgery.

I can't handle this right now. Afon's fury is contagious. Stalking toward the door, I bark over my shoulder at Ruby. "Stay here."

I move faster with every step, and I'm running by the time I reach my car. When I open the door and climb inside, movement from my right makes me glance over. Ruby slams her door shut.

Dammit.

"You need to get back inside." I try to contain my anger, but it's taken over my body, and my words come out in a growl.

She just gives a tiny shake of her head and latches the seat belt.

"Get out, Ruby. You don't want to do this. Fuck." I run a hand through my hair. "I'm serious. Get the fuck out or I'll throw you out. Paco is dead, so I'll make sure to have my lawyer start the divorce proceedings. I'm done."

The woman snorts before she raises one of her groomed eyebrows. "Shut it, Yegor. There's nothing you can throw out that I haven't already heard. You're stuck with me and you know it. Now drive."

"Bitch." I growl.

Fuck. I rip my hand away from the steering wheel due to the pain that brutally slices through it.

"I resent that." Ruby points one finger of her hand that's hovering above the place where my hand was at a second ago. "I might have said there's nothing you can throw out that I haven't already heard, but seriously...don't ever call me a bitch. My husband would spank my ass if I called myself a bitch. Therefore I will slap your hand in return. Even if you don't want to be my..."

"Shut it, Ruby. I get what you're saying." I snap in defeat, although a hint of warmth spreads deep in my chest. She saw me at my worst, and even now when I push her away, she fucking slaps me on the hand.

On the fucking hand. The ones that are swollen

and hurting from beating Paco's face to a pulp. A smile spreads across my face as I pull out of the parking lot.

It might seem like I'm driving around mindlessly, but I'm not. I'm building up to what I need to do. When I pass the cemetery for the fourth time, I finally hit the blinker and pull over. Shutting off the engine, I take a moment to gather my strength.

It's been years since I've been here. Ruby doesn't say anything. It's like she isn't even here, and yet she gives me everything I need to lean on. Nodding to myself, I step out of the car and walk to the grave of my uncle. Even though the exact family tree was never pointed out, I can't hardly blame them since I didn't ask, I knew we weren't related by blood.

My Italian side clearly on the surface. Makes more sense now seeing both of my parents were Italian. My uncle gave me a Russian name when I came to live with him as a kid, adopting me fully. Also the reason growing up, I didn't care much about where I came from, because my uncle made me feel like I belonged.

Paco could have spilled the story right from a crack in his fucked-up brain. Yet somehow it all clicked. I said I didn't care much about my past, but that doesn't mean I never looked into it once or twice. That's why I had a file on Paco...I never knew exactly who my father was. Not one picture. All a fucking spiral of a family vendetta.

A soft touch strokes up my spine. "We're really something, aren't we? Screwed up past...alone without family, and yet together with a whole bunch of folks that would hit us on the backs of our heads if we voiced that we have no family at all. The way I see it...the day you came into my life was the first time I really started to live. Even if it started out like shit...looking back...things might not be so bad. I mean, how much worse can it get, right?"

Spinning around, I take her in my arms and pull her close.

"You have no idea what you do to me." I nuzzle my face into her hair, while I breathe her in.

She's right. Our past, recent events, it all lead up

to this moment, with me holding her close. She's everything I ever needed in life. Just as she pointed out, we have a whole family surrounding us. Hell, our gang, Peacock's, and I'm pretty sure Ricca will back us up, just as we will be there for him.

"I don't have anything but the stories they've told me. What Paco mentioned about my mother... *It's only in death that I respect the last and final thing our mother did*...I respect her for the same reasons and yet completely different. It's a vile, ruthless world that requires strength and utter devotion. No matter how you're brought down or ripped apart, we make our own choices."

I pull back and stare at her amazing eyes, filled with love and respect for me. "I love you, Ruby. I can't imagine my life without you."

"Finally. I was starting to think I'd have to slap you on the hands some more to get through to you." She rolls her eyes as if she's annoyed but her mouth twitches.

Damn, I'm so fucking lucky to have her with me.

I almost fucked it up again when I wanted to push her away. Thank God she wouldn't let me.

My mouth covers hers as I slide my hand into her hair and tighten it to a fist. She gasps as I groan. I slide my tongue against hers, even as my hand throbs like crazy.

Pulling back, my lips hover over hers. "Let's go home. It's been a long day."

"Hmmhmmm. I'm sure the place is squeaky clean by now. Are you up for a hot bath with your knuckles? Or do they need to stay out of the water?" The concern in her eyes is adorable.

She hasn't seen my hands. I've cleaned them up myself and pulled on the gloves because we needed to head over to the hospital. It doesn't matter. They'll heal.

"Are you crazy? I won't give up a hot bath with my woman over some raw and bruised knuckles."

Turning, she grabs my wrist and walks with me back to the car. I grab my phone and shoot a message, because there was one thing my brother was right about. I'm taking his advice, because you learn from some mistakes.

It takes an hour to get home and at least two more hours pass before we're snuggling on the couch. The doorbell rings. Standing, I make my way over, because I know what's coming.

Ruby doesn't get up. We're watching some kind of doctor's series on Netflix, and I'm fine with it. It's relaxing to have my wife in my arms, comfortable, doing nothing. But all of that is about to change.

"Come on in." I tell the man and woman.

When I sent a text to my lawyer, I told her to send over her sister and her husband.

The man holds out his hand. "I'm Peter, this is my wife, Edith. We brought you two, per your request."

I take Peter's hand and give it a firm squeeze. "Thanks. Set them free."

I chuckle, looking at the small pet carrier on the floor. Edith grins and opens the door. Two gray little bundles dart out and head for the living room.

"Wow." Edith looks back at her husband. "They aren't normally this energetic. I mean, they do run and play, but most times they're a little skittish when we bring them somewhere new."

"Oooooooooh…" Ruby gasps from the living room.

"Guess my wife found the surprise I got her…or better yet, the surprise found her." Peter and Edith laugh and I gladly join them, knowing I made the right decision. "Let's follow the puppies so you can tell us all about them."

My lawyer told me that her sister breeds Weimaraners. She had a litter and there were three pups left. I sent her a text that I wanted two. No more sneaking up on me. Even if they manage to shut down my state-of-the-art alarm system, we now have two dogs added to the mix.

When we get to the living room, there's no sign of either the dogs or Ruby. There is, however, a stream of giggles coming from behind the couch. Strolling over, I see my wife on the ground, hugging one of the gray bundles while the other one is pulling her hair with its teeth.

"Having fun with our boys, Ruby?" My cheeks hurt from smiling; it's too damn cute.

She looks up into my eyes and there's so much emotion, I have to place my hand on the couch to keep my knees from buckling.

"They are perfect." She whispers before she scoops up the other pup, gets to her feet, and plants a kiss on my lips. The next moment, I swear two other tongues are added to the mix, making both of us step back.

It's then I realize my life can never get any more perfect than this.

CHAPTER SIXTEEN

Tiptoe with your dick.

Ruby

"Don't eat that, Gus." Ugh.

Bending down, I try to remove what's left of the paper from between Gus' teeth, while Jax watches from a safe distance, tilting his sweet, tiny, velvet puppy head. Well, not so tiny. They're almost six months old already.

"You're just as naughty, you bad, bad, boy." I tell him, and he sinks down to the floor and lays his head on his paws.

He should feel guilty. He's probably sitting on the rest of the fragments of the box the pregnancy test came in.

"I needed those directions, you know." I huff.

But then again…maybe not, because how difficult can it be? Piss on a stick and then what was it, one or two stripes? See…needed it.

"What's going on?"

Yegor's voice makes me yelp. Dammit, I should have locked the bathroom door. That would have saved me from the three guys in my life.

"Nothing." I grumble as I pick the last piece of paper off the floor.

Or so I think because Yegor reaches down and holds up a large chunk. "Nothing, huh?"

Shit.

"Did they devour the test or did you take it already? Are we pregnant?" His head tilts, clearly waiting for an answer.

"How the hell should I know?" I seethe. "I peed on the freaking stick, only to walk back to the bedroom to discover the boys had grabbed the box and eaten half of it. I had to chase them around and pull pieces of it from Gus' teeth, and I really needed the box, because I don't know how to read the damn thing and…"

"Ruby." Yegor spills my name from his lips, and it's like a soft caress, relaxing me immediately. "Where is the test?"

I point behind me, and he walks over to grab it from the sink. He stares at it for a second or two before he puts it back down, his expression blank.

"Well?" I ask, my hands coming up on each side of my body, holding them palms up.

"Well…" He stalks toward me and takes me in his arms. "I'm thinking it will be a boy. But I want a girl too. We've got enough room, so I'm sure we could try…"

Leaning to my right, I look around him at the stick. Two lines. "Oh. Two lines mean pregnant. I wanted to double check but…"

"No need to double check, Ruby. This belly," He places his hand possessively over my abdomen. "Is carrying our child."

"Gonna be a real daddy."

"And you'll be a real mommy."

"So we have a few months to get these monsters under control because apparently we failed somewhere in raising them." I grumble when I look back at two enormously cute dogs.

"We'll be fine. Here, I'll show you." Yegor gives me a kiss on my neck before he snaps his fingers. "Gus, Jax, out."

Both boys dart out of the bathroom and head for the bedroom door. Yegor closes it behind them and turns to me.

"See, no problem." There's a smug smile on his face. "It's time for me to worship that body of yours. Especially now that it just became even more special."

I feel my cheeks heat at his words, while warmth spreads inside my chest. This man. He completes me.

Before he can throw out a command he wants me to follow, I take lead and stalk toward him. Dropping to my knees in front of him, I reach for his belt.

His erection is already straining against the zipper of his slacks.

Yegor's eyes burn into mine, swirling with dark desire. His slacks hit the floor, freeing his dick that is reaching for his navel. Thick and hard. Wrapping my fingers around the soft, veiny skin, I slide my tongue over the tip. I taste the salty fluid that leaks out.

It's then that I feel his hand sliding in my hair, guiding my cheek toward his thigh. This reminds me of the first time I had his cock in my mouth. The way he takes control, the way he fucks my mouth. Always his way. Yet this man goes out of his way to do anything for me. Placing my needs first.

Except when it comes to blowjobs. I can take control when we have sex, straddle him, determine the pace, and get him off with my hand. But the second my mouth comes near his dick, he places my cheek on his thigh and wraps his inked-up hand around his girth to pump fiercely until he spills everything he has down my throat.

It's hot. Sometimes all I need is one brush of my own fingers over my clit to orgasm right after him.

It's like he gains control over both our bodies when he merges my cheek with his thigh, his dick with my mouth, our eyes locked.

"You're not going to get it down your throat this time, gorgeous." Yegor tells me, his voice pained. "I want to be deep inside you, feeling that pussy pulse from the orgasm I'll give you. I want to kiss those lips you so expertly wrapped around me. Get up, Ruby. On the bed."

See? Like I mentioned earlier…he throws out commands and expect me to follow them. Well, it seems like he holds the remote that goes to my body, because he knows exactly what buttons to push.

The place between my legs starts to throb in anticipation of what's to come. Shrugging off my clothes, I place a knee on the bed and look over my shoulder.

"Ass on the bed, I want to look at my pussy, have a taste before I crawl up and slide in." He toes off his shoes and slacks and unbuttons his shirt.

Propping myself on my elbows, I take in the man who holds my heart. With powerful strides he guides his muscled body toward me. His tattoos are scattered over his skin. A large chest piece, flowing onto his arms, forearms, and his hand. My mouth is dry, probably because of the extended drooling I had going just now. It's too much.

"Do you want me to stand here some more, so you can eye fuck me before I fuck you?" He takes his dick in hand and starts to stroke himself.

My hand slides down, heading between my legs because he's right. I really could eye fuck him, all it would take is one touch...

"Don't you dare touch my pussy. The only one who will come near that bundle of nerves is me with my tongue, my fingers, and my cock. Clear?" He growls as his knee hits the mattress.

Leaning over, his tongue slides over my pussy, my clit, over my belly, latching on to my nipple and biting down. I feel his cock pressing against me as his fingers snake underneath my leg, locking my knee with his arm, opening me up as he slides my leg over his shoulder. Raising his knee, he cradles my other leg between his as he buries his cock inside me.

Grunting loudly, he pulls back. I fully expect for him to slam back in and yet he takes his time, as if savoring our connection. My walls clench around him when he's all the way in, right before he moves back.

His voice is a low, deep rumble. "Ruby. I'm going slow here, don't make me hurt you."

I gasp, digging my nails into his shoulders. "Okay, mister maybe I didn't know how to read a pregnancy test, but this I do know…you can't hurt the baby or me by the way we've been fucking. Don't you dare start to tiptoe with your dick."

"Tiptoe with my dick, Ruby? Really?"

Before I can answer, he starts to pound into me, taking away all bodily functions.

The only thing I can do is surrender to the pleasure he's building for release. His mouth latches onto the skin of my neck. Yegor's hand cups my chin and guides my head to the side for better access. I can feel his dick start to swell even more before it pulses inside me. He rotates his pelvis and I'm lost. Tingles erupt throughout my body as the most intense orgasm overtakes me.

I groan in frustration when I hear my iPhone buzz on the bedside table. Pulling me out of my moment. Yegor slips out of me, leaving me to repeat the frustrated sound. I watch as his tight, sculpted, ass strolls over to the bathroom before I reach for my phone.

It's a text from Andy. A warm cloth hits between my legs, and I yelp in shock.

"Touchy, touchy. This new?" Yegor chuckles.

I smack his biceps as he keeps cleaning my pussy. "No, you idiot. I was reading a text from Andy."

His hand pulls back and he throws the wet cloth in the direction of the bathroom. I'm glad to see it hit the tiled floor instead of the carpet.

"What did it say? Where is she?" His face is fierce.

Andy spent some time in the hospital, and after that she needed time to regain strength in her shoulder. But she vanished barely three days after she was taken to the hospital. Ricca freaked out, but she let us girls know that she checked herself into a private clinic. She sent a text to her brother to let him know she needed time.

He wasn't thrilled but understood. Something about her past, except neither Ricca nor Andy will spill a word about it. Her brother was pissed she removed the GPS chip in her arm. But then again it's not like you're giving a person space when you can pinpoint her location every time you like, right?

Yegor knows us girls keep in contact with Andy, but he also knows not to ask too much or that I can't tell him some things. Mainly because Afon left the same day Andy did.

They didn't run off together. On the contrary, Afon is chasing down Marco. Apparently, Marco took almost half his brother's gang, well it's Marco's gang now, with him. I can't tell Yegor that Andy is chasing down Marco too. That I just got a message in our girl group chat that she's about to close in on him.

Because then all hell would break loose, right? He keeps staring at me intently, clearly expecting me to tell him something.

My phone rings. Checking the screen, I recognize the number and pick up the call. "Hey Andy!"

There's nothing but breathing on the other side of the line.

"Hello?" A male's voice cracks over the phone. "Who is this?"

"Ruby. Who's this?" I ask.

There's static, and then the voice comes back, repeating the same. "Who is this?"

"It's Yegor's bitch, now who are you?" I snap.

Yegor growls low in his throat and bends forward, bringing our heads together. "Your ass is gonna feel that one." He whispers close to my ear.

The voice in my other ear now comes clearly over my phone. "Ah, Yegor's bitch. Let him know I'm coming to avenge my brother. And I'll start with the girly brunette one of my men just grabbed."

The line goes dead...my heart starts to pound

as my eyes lock on Yegor who clearly heard the same words.

My whole body starts to shake. "No!" I gasp.

The Dudnik Circle will return
with Afon's story.

THANKS!

My beta team;

Rebecca, Cathy, Neringa, Tracy, Judy,

my pimp team (especially Neringa) and to you,

as my reader, and let's not forget my editor…

Thanks so much! You guys rock!

Contact:

I love hearing from my readers.

Email:

authoresthereschmidt@gmail.com

Or contact my PA **Christi Durbin** for any questions you might have. facebook.com/CMDurbin

ESTHER E. SCHMIDT

Visit Esther E. Schmidt online:

Website:
www.esthereschmidt.nl

Facebook - AuthorEstherESchmidt
Twitter - @esthereschmidt
Instagram - @esthereschmidt
Pinterest - @esthereschmidt

Signup for Esther's newsletter:
esthereschmidt.nl/newsletter

Join Esther's fan group on Facebook:
www.facebook.com/groups/estherselite

Join The Swamp Heads group on Facebook:
www.facebook.com/groups/TheSwampHeadsSeries

MORE BOOKS
BY
ESTHER E. SCHMIDT

Areion Fury MC Series

Zack (Areion Fury MC #1)

Dams (Areion Fury MC #2)

Tyler (Areion Fury MC #3)

Pokey (Areion Fury MC #4) – COMING SOON

Sico (Areion Fury MC #5) – COMING SOON

Calix (Areion Fury MC #6) – COMING SOON

Broken Deeds MC

Deeds (Broken Deeds MC #1)

Broke (Broken Deeds MC #2)

Depay (Broken Deeds MC #3)

Ramrod (Broken Deeds MC #4) – COMING SOON

Lochlan (Broken Deeds MC #5) – COMING SOON

Wicked Throttle MC

Corban (Wicked Throttle MC #0.5)

Xerox (Wicked Throttle MC MC #1) 2017

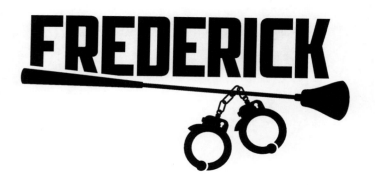

The Dudnik Circle

Ford (The Dudnik Circle #1)

Yegor (The Dudnik Circle #2)

Afon (The Dudnik Circle #3) – COMING SOON

PEACOCK

THE FAULTS OF OUR SINS

NEON MARKSMAN MC

29351545R00151

Printed in Great Britain
by Amazon